STRANGE TALES IN BRADFORD DALE

Irene Lofthouse

Gizmo Publications

STRANGE TALES IN BRADFORD DALE

Published 2015

Copyright © Irene Lofthouse 2015

All rights reserved

Cover design and illustrations by Clare Lindley

Gizmo Publications

www.gizmo.co.uk

ISBN 978-1-900827-54-6

Printed and bound in the UK by 4edge Limited

Reviews for Book 1 *Strange Tales in the Dales*

"Scary but fun." *Grace, 8, The Grinning Gargoyle*

"That was well spooky." *Matthew, 9, The Headless Horseman*

"The stories are really exciting and you never know what's going to happen next." *Daisy, 7*

"I like the stories, they make me want to read more." *Hamid, 10*

"The Necklace is my favourite. I feel I'm on the train with Jack." *Jasmine, 11*

"Loved the book. I read half of it in bed the other night and was really spooked!! In a good way..." *Emma Clayton, Telegraph & Argus*

"The book looks great and definitely fills a gap in the market for local myths and legends." *Caroline Brown, Local Studies Manager, Bradford*

"Irene is a great storyteller." *Librarian, North Yorks*

"This has been [a] great [event]. We can do lots of follow-on work from it." *KS2 teacher, Catterick*

"Just brilliant. The best praise I can give this book is not that it is wildly imaginative (which it is), or that the stories are just the perfect length for kids to read at a single sitting (which they are), or that the tales themselves are exciting and superbly written (which they are). The best praise I can give it is that it turned my 12 year old son, previously a reluctant reader, into an avid reader who not only devoured the book in double-quick time, but then asked if there were any more books like this that he could read. That's some achievement, believe me, and we'll be first in the queue for Strange Tales Vol 2." *Mark, Australia*

About the Author

Irene has been telling tales been telling stories since she was little – her school reports prove it. As writer, storyteller and actor she's continued to do so at festivals, events, theatres and on radio, TV and film for many years. Irene works with schools, museums, galleries, community groups, historic and art organisations on a variety of heritage and creative projects.

When she's writing, Georgia the old cat keeps her company and if she gets stuck, Irene goes for walks to ruined abbeys, through ancient woods and along the river with Tully her hound, until she's unstuck.

www.word-sauce.com

Introduction

Bradford has a fascinating history going back to Neolithic times. But often, people only think about its industrial past. As a Bradford lass at school, I heard stories about medieval manors, hidden tunnels, the legend of the last wild boar, civil war sieges, hauntings, phantoms, witches and magic, amongst others.

When I was young, we bought a book from Readers' Digest called *'Folklore, Myths and Legends of Great Britain'* which had lots of stories about Bradford and it fascinated me. I still have it and revisited it for inspiration for some of the stories here. I take full responsibility for any errors, new characters, time-shifts, different takes on old tales and being creative with story-lines.

There are so many terrific tales, legends, myths and historic happenings that I could have written a huge book, but I'd probably still be writing it. So I've had to pick and choose what to include, focussing on some of Bradford's lesser-known stories, strange and spooky happenings.

Which means there are lots more to revisit in the future.

Irene Lofthouse
September 2015

To all the children who've helped to shape the stories and suggested new ones

Preface

Long ago Broad Ford (as Bradford was known in the Domesday Book) was a heavily forested dale threaded through with many becks which joined the one that runs in front of St Peter's Church, (Bradford Cathedral). Bradford Beck (now underground) and the waterways were important to the woollen trade that grew in the area and may have been used to wash wool for centuries by the different people who settled here.

Celts, Norse, Angles, Danes, Roman, Normans, Irish, Asians, Africans and more have crossed the land as migrants, invaders, soldiers and slaves. They brought myths, legends, rites and stories with them, sometimes creating new ones or gave old ones new names and twists.

I've done something similar in this collection, re-imagining and re-telling old tales and myths, inventing new ones based on legends, personal experience, the landscape and architecture.

All the places mentioned in the tales can be visited, so you can make up your own minds about their 'strangeness' and may even have your own 'spooky' experience.

Contents   Page

The Boar's Severed Head

I

"Hurry up!" Ranulf crashed through the trees surrounding the hamlet, shouting at anyone he saw. "It's coming this way!" Get your livestock in! Shut up your chickens and barricade your doors!"

Although Ranulf was only ten, everyone rushed around following his orders. They ran to bring in cows from grazing and led them into the small cottages they called home.

Children chased after flapping chickens, whilst older ones attempted to stop roosters crowing. Mothers picked up crawling babies, bundling them tightly before putting them in rough-hewn cots.

All was done as silently as possible. The usual banter and cursing as people went about their daily life was missing. Only heavy breathing from their exertions could be heard. But the smell of fear floated on the breeze.

Ranulf helped his sister, Aleycia to put their animals away, which didn't take long having only a goat and some chickens. She was tying a rag around the goat's mouth to keep it quiet. Ranulf kept his eyes bright and watchful on the woods around them, his ear cocked for noise. He held a pitchfork in his hands.

He knew it would happen one day, that he'd be the eldest male in the hamlet. This was the day. All the menfolk were out in the fields tending to the crops, thinking it safe now to venture out.

"I have it on good authority it's moved away," his father had said last night. "We need to make sure the crops are growing. We haven't been to the fields for over two weeks and they could all be dead."

"But if you go out, you could be the one to end up dead." Aleycia's mouth had wobbled as she said this. A year younger than Ranulf, she'd had to grow up and take on the woman's role when their mother had died. The thought of her father being killed was more than she could bear.

"It hasn't been seen anywhere in t'woods from St Peter's to here for more than a month," her father said. "I'm sure it's moved away. There's better pickings in the King's hunting grounds than here with our scrawny goat. I'll be fine." He'd hugged Aleycia reassuringly.

"The sons of Radolphus, David and Elyas will be here," he continued. "They're all skilled bowmen and handy with a knife. You've got nothing to worry about."

II

Ranulf recalled those words as he looked about him. Women's faces peered from under the sacking that covered windows. Young ones, some newly married, widows and old Agnes. Where where the young men left to defend them? They'd taken themselves off to the nearest hostelry, making the most of their fathers' absence.

A noise in the undergrowth caught his attention. He concentrated on the direction it had come from, his eyes searching for movement, his nose quivering trying to detect a specific scent. Everything was quiet apart from the droning of the bees as they buzzed amongst the flowers and bushes.

There! He heard it again, only louder this time. He gripped the pitchfork tighter. Ranulf wasn't sure what he was going to do, but he knew he had to do something. Why hadn't his father trained him with a bow? He wasn't too young, he had good eyesight - SQUAWCK!

Birds rose in a mass from the trees, cawing, screeching, creating a racket. Underneath it, was the sound of heavy hooves trampling the ground, a loud grunting and snarling that had rabbits and hares speeding past Ranulf as if he wasn't there.

Erupting from the trees came a massive boar. Saliva dripped red from the creatures it had recently devoured. Sharp tusks gleamed whitely in the sunshine. Beady eyes fixed themselves on the lone boy by the well in the middle of the hamlet.

Ranulf felt his throat tighten, his hands ooze sweat, his heartbeat increase and an overwhelming desire to turn and run. He saw the boar's nose twitch, sniffing, sensing fear in the smell of sweat carried on the breeze. Rooted to the spot, Ranulf's body tensed as the enormous animal lowered its head – a sure sign it was about to charge.

Its gaze shifted suddenly, ears pricking at the sound of a whimper from the cottages. A split second was all it took for Ranulf to hurl himself at the boar whilst it was distracted. Shouting, screaming, making as much noise as possible, he ran forward, pitchfork thrust out like a spear.

Behind him, the villagers joined their shouting voices to his, banging loudly on whatever they could to disorient the ravaging beast. Rushing forward, the boy could see confusion in the boar's movements; ears flicking to and fro, eyes darting around showing it wasn't as ready to attack as it had been.

Thrusting the pitchfork in front as he got closer, Ranulf shouted, "Go on! Get away! Go!" He was acting braver than he felt. His legs were like the savoury jelly his mum used to make, his mouth as dry as a well in a drought, his heart as tight as the skin on a drum.

"Please," he pleaded in his head, jabbing forward again, eyes fixed on the boar, "please, just go!"

He was within three feet of the boar and could smell its rancid breath when the boar raised its head. A growl like rumbling thunder issued from its red mouth, stopping a jab mid-thrust. Ranulf felt his bladder begin to loosen. He hoped he wouldn't shame himself when the beast charged. He didn't want to die, but knew his pitchfork was no match for this killing machine.

Trying to stay calm for his sister and villagers, Ranulf shouted at the boar again. "We don't want you here. Go to the deer park, where there's plenty of meat and leave us alone!" Closing his eyes, the boy poked his pitchfork in the direction of the beast, waiting for it to charge.

III

Nothing happened. Opening his blue eyes, Ranulf found himself alone near the edge of the forest. The boy looked around, bewildered. All was quiet except for the droning bees.

Shrieks of joy erupted from the cottages as children and women holding babies ran from their hiding places. Aleycia was the first to reach her brother, grabbing him so hard he nearly fell. Tears ran down her face as she sobbed and gabbled.

"Ranulf! I thought it was going to kill you! You're so brave! Wait until father hears. Surely he'll let you train as an archer now! Oh Ranulf!" Sobbing again, she hugged him.

The women praised his courage and agreed with Aleycia about how proud his father would be now the village was safe.

"But it's not safe!" Ranulf declared "Summat must have frightened it. It'll be back. We can't celebrate yet."

"Quite right little Ranulf," a voice behind them said. "'Boar's only interested where there's sows roaming free."

In the hubbub, the elders' sons had arrived without anyone noticing. Elfric, Radolphus's son, a blond-haired lad of slim stature continued. "It's what John Northrop said not an hour ago."

"And where did he say that? In t'hostelry?" Agnes mimicked drinking with her hand. "Where you lot went, abandoning yer womenfolk, while we wait, wondering if we're t'be gored by t'ravaging boar?" Flicking a greasy grey plait over her shoulder, Agnes stood, arms folded.

A second youth, smaller than his friends shook his head,

his freckled face and red hair showing his Norman roots.

"No-one knew it was so near, as Ranulf's father said," Alun explained, "but it's moved rapidly in the last couple of days."

"Northrop told a tale," Ludus, a dark-haired youth broke in, "about a happening in Ide's forest. Two newborn babes disappeared one night and haven't been found. Only the torn blood-soaked swaddling cloths in a clearing."

This silenced everyone. Ide's forest was only a few hours walk away on a track from their hamlet in Cliff Wood. Possibly the track the boar had taken. Mothers clutched their babies tighter, looking around, afraid.

"The boar also attacked Roger de Manningham's sows," continued Ludus. "Everyone's angry that the Lord of the Manor's not doing anything."

"Aye well, that'll be 'cos he dunt live among us," Agnes commented. "Just 'cos he owns t'land, dunt mean he knows what's going on."

"He'll do summat quick enough if his livestock and hunting's threatened," Ranulf pointed out.

"Right again. Smart aren't you?" Ranulf scowled at Elfric, recognising a sarcastic remark. Aleycia frowned. She longed for the day when Ranulf wiped away their smug smiles.

"Smart enough t'see off a boar whilst you left us unguarded. What'll your fathers say to that I wonder?" Aleycia's pertness made Agnes grin. The youths began to bluster when Agnes cut them off, pointing to the track.

"We'll soon find out. Here they come."

IV

That evening Alfred called everyone to a meeting. The elders sat next to him, the villagers sat on the hard dirt floor. Mothers held children on their knees, hounds snuffled around, a fire burned in a corner fed with branches by two young lads in dun-coloured tunics and dirty feet.

In her thread-bare kirtle, Agnes pounded herbs for a salve near the open door to catch the fading light. Alfred reproved Alun, Elfric and Ludus for their absence.

"But they found out that the boar's closer then we thought," Radolphus said.

"And if they'd been here, they could have killed it and we'd be safe!" Alfred snapped.

"If Ranulf had a bow, he could have killed it," Aleycia

piped up, "or a hunting knife -." She stopped, silenced by the angry looks from both her brother and father, hiding her red face in her coif. Ranulf tried to shrink as Elfric's eyes bored into him.

"Lass is reet," Agnes said, "Question is, what do we do? We can't live in fear, wondering if animals or babies will be teken and killed."

Everyone had a suggestion, talking over each other about sentries, patrols, traps and pits, guarding the livestock. Alfred raised his hands for silence. "All very sensible, but we have work and crops t'see to." Turning to the quiet youths, he asked, "Did Northrop and de Manningham have a plan of action?"

Elfric, a little red-faced, spoke first. "Northrop thought archers should search for the boar."

"But de Manningham said there should be a reward." Ludus stood as he spoke

"From the Lord of the Manor," Alun added. "He said we should go to Bolling and voice our grievances."

"Good idea," Agnes said over her shoulder. "It's his responsibility t'keep the land safe fer folks."

Alfred sighed. It was best not to cross Agnes when she

offered an opinion being, as she was, a powerful cunning woman who'd saved many lives. Everyone stayed quiet as Alfred wondered what to do. The sound of running feet broke the silence. A panting cottar skidded into view, dirt streaking his face, blood on his hands, shouting, "Boar's got a cow!"

The elders were on their feet in an instant and Alfred grabbed the man's blood-stained tunic. "How did it get in? T'byre doors were secured."

"I don't know sir," the cottar stammered. "I walked past the byre and noticed a trail of blood on the ground. I followed it round the back, there was a hole, more blood and a cow missing inside."

Uproar ensued. Women hugged their children closely, fear making them hurry home to barricade them into a safe space.

"'So, does tha tek threat o'boar seriously now then?" Agnes's stern voice asked.

"Aye Agnes, we do and we need t'decide what to do." Radolphus answered.

"Well you'd best mek yer minds up quick then," the old woman replied, sitting down ready to debate.

V

On the morrow, the elders and their sons set off to join de Manningham's deputation to Bolling. Alfred, Ranulf and the cottars went to search for the missing cow. Aleycia's task was to collect herbs with Agnes who couldn't crouch to pick them.

"Dunt worry lass, you'll be safe wi' me," Agnes grinned as they walked into the wood. "Boar'll tek one look at my scrawny body an' ignore us. And," she paused, holding up a finger, "I've put a spell on us so we're invisible."

Aleycia believed it and followed quietly behind. It was warm work digging up roots, picking flowers and a variety of herbs for salves, lotions and food flavouring. Soon Agnes decided it was time for a rest.

"We'll head t'Spinkwell for a drink," she said. "It's sweet, cool, fresh *and* has niver run dry, not even in droughts. We can tek our ease wi' bread an' cheese."

They sat in the shade munching food whilst bees droned in the bramble flowers. After a while, Aleycia heard another drone, then realised it was Agnes snoring.

Being young and full of energy, the girl decided to stretch

her legs. Humming as she wandered, she soon found herself at another well and pool where she heard more snoring.

Across the pool on its side, was the boar, fast asleep. Aleycia held her breath for what seemed like ages, before walking softly away casting looks over her shoulder to make sure the boar wasn't following.

VI

Meanwhile Alfred told the cottars to scour the hill for the cow in small groups and to look for blood or droppings. Armed with daggers and bows they fanned out. Skilled at hunting, the men made little noise as they crept through the undergrowth.

A movement caught Ranulf's eye. They were in a dense part of the woods but the rustling of leaves got Alfred's attention too. He pointed, putting one finger to his lips, whilst signalling them forward with his other hand.

Each man had an arrow in place, ready to loose it at any animal that ran past. Ranulf was frustrated that all he had was a dagger. Everyone edged closer to the rustling. Alfred signalled a halt. He was about to step forward when out came the boar, trotting as if on a woodland stroll. Catching the men's scent, it gave a mighty growl and lunged at Alfred.

"Father!" Ranulf cried. The boar immediately changed direction toward the boy, who stood dagger in hand, fear etched on his face. The cottars froze as the boar moved. An arrow from Alfred's bow grazed the boar's back making it grunt and plunge away from them into the woods.

Ranulf's hand shook. Striding over, Alfred lifted his son's chin and looked into his eyes. "You alright?"

Ranulf swallowed, blinking. "Yes sir."

Alfred nodded. Turning to the cottars, he blasted them. "Call yerself men? If you don't shape up, that boar'll have us for its dinner!" He strode angrily into the clearing.

The cow's remains were strewn around. "Leave it here," Alfred ordered, "and boar'll return." He blew a piercing whistle, the signal for the search parties to head back.

VII

Excitement rose in the hamlet when the groups began to return. Agnes and Aleycia arrived first, going to the cottage to hang herbs.

Next to come were the elders. Their sons were full of themselves, desperate for someone to ask what had happened, but no one did. Tension grew as the search parties began to arrive, sharing stories and food with the women.

Into this strode Alfred and his party. Chattering hushed at the sight of their bloodstained clothes. Aleycia ran to her brother as everyone waited for Alfred to speak.

"T'boar has begun t'devour cow," Alfred announced. "When it's hungry, it'll be back. I'll choose the best of the hunters -,"

Ludus, Alun and Elfric interrupted, shouted that it wasn't his decision to make.

"Silence!" Alfred barked. "What do you mean I can't make t'decision? I'm -," This time Elyas interrupted.

"We saw Bolling and told him of the ravaging, killing and the t'terror. Rishworth and Northrop said t'same thing."

The older boys shouted again but Elyas held up his hand.

"Bolling has issued a proclamation offering a reward of land for any man who kills t'boar and brings him evidence."

"And those old enough to be an archer have the right to hunt the boar! Like us!" Ludus and Elfric grinned proudly.

Aleycia saw Ranulf's frustrated face. Agnes saw the

fearful faces of their mothers as they imagined wounds and worse. Alfred saw the hungry looks of the cottars. Owning your own land was what everyone dreamed of.

"It's good that Bolling has listened," Alfred said. "But every man across t'Wapentake will be chasin' t'reward. We can't have every man from here hunting at t'same time."

"But you can't stop us!" Alun cried.

"I won't. A dead boar is good for all of us, but we must be able to guard our hamlet. Let's all rest and I'll come up with a plan."

VIII

The next morning Alfred shared his idea. A list would be drawn up so that archers had an equal chance until the boar was slain. The men and youths cheered, jostling to follow Alfred and sign their names.

Several days later, Aleycia and Ranulf decided to go to find the cow and see if they could track the boar. No sighting of it had been made by the men, so the siblings thought it was now or never. When their father went to milk the cows, they set off, both with knives from the kitchen. Agnes saw them but decided to say nothing. She was knew they'd come to no harm.

As they walked along, Aleycia picked berries, their excuse for being in the wood. Ranulf kept his eyes and ears open. Quite soon, a crashing sound made them dash into a thicket for cover. Peeping through the hawthorn, they saw two youths, arms flailing, come hurtling down the incline, feet hardly touching the ground.

Pitching forward onto the track, sobbing and crying, legs covered with scratches, breath coming in ragged spurts, the youths looked up, squeaking. "Nooo!" Leaping up, they set off down the track in the direction of the hiding children, running for all they were worth. Clearly frightened, hair wild, Ludus and Elfric flew past. Aleycia and Ranulf gripped their knives tightly, sure that the boar was coming, their throats dry and hearts pounding.

Small rocks rolled down the hillside stopping as a long furry body landed with a thud. A greyhound streaked by chased by a man in a green tunic whistling furiously. He had a bow in one hand, quiver on his back and a broken leash in his other hand.

Aleycia and Ranulf burst out laughing. Ludus and Elfric!

running away from a hound! So much for the 'brave' youths!

"I don't think we'll see the boar after that racket," Aleycia said crawling out of the thicket. "We'd best get going. Father will be suspicious if we're not there when the boys get back."

IX

Agnes was tying a bandage around Ludus's left wrist when the children returned. Elfric's mother tutted at him, spreading salves across his arms.

"Are you sure it was t'boar?" Elyas asked.

"Yes sir," Elfric replied. "It was big and ferocious with a very loud growl and -,"

"It chased us through the woods," Ludus interrupted, "we didn't have time for bows, but we managed to throw stones so we could escape."

"That was no boar!" Aleycia laughed out loud. Ludus and Elfric reddened as the crowd's eyes flicked between them and Aleycia.

"Explain yourself!" her father demanded.

Opening her bag, showing the berries, she explained what had happened. "They were nowhere near a boar!" she finished.

"Is this true?" Elfric's mother and father demanded. The boys' lips quivered, their heads down avoiding any eye contact.

"Answer them!" Alfred's voice boomed. The crowd watched as the boys squirmed.

"We thought, we thought it was a boar," Ludus stammered, "it's jaws were open and foaming – oww!" He gave a yelp as Agnes pulled the bandage tightly.

Elyas yanked Elfric from his place, dragging him away, whispering angrily in his ear. His mother followed, avoiding neighbours' eyes.

Alfred announced, "There'll be no more hotheaded youths of fourteen hunting, whatever Bolling says."

"Are you going t'hunt it father?" Ranulf asked hesitantly. Everyone had wondered, because Alfred's name wasn't on the list.

"No," he said emphatically. "If I was killed who'd look after you? I'll leave it t'others. This is our home."

Aleycia breathed a sigh of relief. She was glad her father wasn't going to hunt, she didn't want to be an orphan.

X

No hunters had spotted the boar that day either. On his return, Ludus's father David heard what had happened and his son's scratches were soon joined by several bruises. Alun was angry to find out that he couldn't hunt due to his friends' lies.

Tension continued in the hamlet throughout the week. Agnes watched families fall out with each other as the chase for the prize of land and betterment took hold. She decided that something had to be done.

She approached Alfred. "We need more herbs," she said. "I need Aleycia's nimble fingers t'pick them. T'salves are almost used up. And some protection. Lad's handy wi' a dagger, as well as being fleet of foot."

Alfred raised his eyebrows. "Ranulf's only ten. Tek one of t'older lads. They're trained and they've learned their lesson."

But Agnes was insistent. She wanted reliable helpers not sulky youths. As usual, she got her way and it wasn't long before she and the children set off.

Once the woods hid the hamlet, Agnes stopped and unpinned her long cloak. To astonished eyes she revealed a bow and quiver held over her shoulders.

"I've seen you wi' your home-made one and you're pretty good." The boy's mouth opened and closed like a fish. "Give your sister t'dagger, she knows what t'do wi' one," continued the cunning woman. "We're going t'sort this boar business once an' for all. Come on."

Reaching the Spinkwell, Agnes stopped. "Down there's where t'boar drinks. We're going to mek sure that any hunter comin' by today teks evidence of a dead boar t'Lord O'Manor. Then we can all get back to our lives."

"But how?" Ranulf and Aleycia were confused.

"I dropped a hint or two about t'boar's well in de Manningham, Northrop, Rishworth and cottars' ears. One of 'em must have sense t'work me hints out."

"But how do we fit in?" Aleycia asked.

"I've brought a sleeping draught for t'boar's drinkin' water. When it's deep asleep, we'll kill it."

The children gasped. If it was that easy, why hadn't Agnes done this with their father?

"I needed to mek sure where it drank and how much I'd need t'mek it sleep," she responded when they asked. "Besides, I thought someone would've killed by now.

Follow!"

Stepping quietly, they made their way to the well. Agnes unstopped her bottle, pouring the liquid into the pool. Then wriggling into the undergrowth, she covered them all with her cloak, leaving an opening so they could watch the path.

Agnes had timed it well. Very soon, lumbering to the pool from their right came the boar. It lapped noisily, the water dribbling from its jaws. Eventually, it laid down with a few grunts, then became quiet.

Breathing rapidly, the children tried to still their anxiety. What if the potion didn't work? What if it heard them?

Agnes whispered, "Now!" and they scrambled from their hiding place, Agnes going to the boar, squinting in its face, lifting eyelids. She straightened up, smiling.

"So, me brave hunters, shall we kill it?"

Aleycia and Ranulf trembled, unsure. It felt different now it was real. Agnes cocked her head, waiting. "I reckon we've got about half an hour before it stirs," she said. "I can't do it on me own. It's now or niver."

Brother and sister looked at each other. "We've killed chickens and rabbits," Aleycia said. "This is just bigger – and it won't move." Ranulf nodded. Agnes smiled, took a dagger from her bag and plunged it into the boar's heart.

"Shoot some arrows," she said, wiping the dagger with her kirtle. "It's what t'hunters will do. T'boar won't wake, potion's done its job."

With help from Aleycia, Ranulf got enough tension on the bow to shoot several arrows deep into the boar's back. Agnes pulled them out, wiped them, and put them back in the quiver.

"Aleycia, get yer dagger out. Can you cut off its tongue so we can tek it back? It's a great delicacy and I think we should have summat to celebrate with."

Gagging on the foul breath and unable to avoid the blood seeping from the arrow holes, Aleycia began to hack at the tongue as Ranulf and Agnes held the mouth wide. It was hard, slippy work with blood and saliva dribbling down the girl's hand. She'd almost got all the way through when an urgent "Shush!" from Agnes had them all still.

"Time to go," Agnes whispered. "Leave t'tongue, no time t'finish it. Follow that small track." She pointed through the trees to a faint path and within minutes, they'd been swallowed up by the wood. Behind them they heard a "Thank the good Lord!" as someone arrived at the dead boar.

XI

Agnes took them to a shepherd's hut in the woods near a small stream where she made them strip and wash before supplying them with a copy of their clothing. Their old ones were burning on a fire. Nothing could amaze brother and sister after what had happened, so they just did as Agnes asked.

"When we get back, Aleycia'll help me as usual. Ranulf, you'll do some wood splitting. No words t'anyone. Just remember you've both saved t'hamlet from danger and strife."

Kicking dirt over the dying fire, Agnes led them back to the hamlet along unknown paths. Arriving back, they quietly carried out their chores whilst their father chatted with Agnes.

As dusk fell, a flushed and breathless cottar arrived in the hamlet, shouting, "It's dead! The boar's dead! We're all safe!" People ran from doorways, cheering. Alfred silenced them.

"Let the man talk. How do you know it's dead?"

Agnes stilled in her work, gesturing to the children to sit.

Dancing with excitement, the cottar repeated what he'd

heard in the town. How de Manningham had arrived on a horse with the boar's bloody head, claiming the land. How Rishworth appeared saying he'd killed the boar. How Bolling had laughed at the claim, but gasped when he saw the boar's bloody tongue in Rishworth's hand. How Bolling threw de Manningham in a dungeon and gave the land at Hunt Yard to Rishworth instead. How some said that it was really Northrop who killed the boar and Rishworth had knocked him out and run off with the tongue.

The villagers whooped with delight at the twists and turns, fetching food and drink for the cottar who would dine out on the story for years to come.

Agnes and the children listened agog. The claim by the men that they had slain the boar was what Agnes expected; but Aleycia and Ranulf were outraged that none of the men had admitted it was dead when they found it.

"But if they said that, no one would get the land," Agnes explained, "and the prize of land was more tempting than the truth." She saw them trying to come to terms with this fact and sighed. It was harder for them to handle than killing the boar. They had grown up a lot in the last few days, she thought. A voice behind her summoned the children.

"I think it's time to turn in," Alfred said. "It'll be a long day tomorrow celebrating. Time for bed."

He was right. The children's eyelids were drooping despite efforts to keep them open. All the fear, tension and excitement had worn them out. Agnes and Alfred picked up the children and skirting the gossiping villagers, they walked to the family's cottage.

"We need summat really special at tomorrow's feast," Alfred said as Agnes turned to go. "I'll leave that in your hands."

Stepping through the door, she nodded, saying to herself, "Shame about that tongue."

A Boggart in the Beck

I

If you were travelling through Bradford Dale several hundred years ago you would have seen many small woollen mills alongside the becks and rivers owned by Abbeys, the Lord of the Manor and wealthy families.

Lots of children from the age of five upwards worked in the mills, sometimes for twelve hours a day for very little money and perhaps one or two days off a year. Small bodies were good to crawl under looms to clean waste wool and small fingers were best to piece broken threads together.

Water was needed for the making of woollens, to clean the fleeces by scouring them to take out any grease, oils and dirt. The Romans used stale urine or the soapwort plant to do this. By medieval times these were replaced by fuller's earth. In big tubs, workers would trample the cloth with their feet before rinsing in the becks.

It was a hard life even before the Industrial Revolution, especially if it was a mill with lots of punishments and fines for not being on time or not getting work done fast enough.

At one such mill, the children were so tired all the time that they began to dream about and wish for a magical helping hand.

II

Unbeknown to them, the site of their mill had been the home of a brownie for centuries. Snuggling down in his hidey-hole along the bank, he'd been there as people came and went. He watched as the mill was built, then the cottages around it. As long as people hadn't bothered him, he hadn't bothered them, content to live alongside until he felt he was needed.

Now he listened with interest to the voices discussing what life would be like with a magical friend.

"If we wished 'ard enough, we could summon a fairy!" Edie's eyes sparkled as she swept the floor.

"But fairies dunt do 'ard work like us," said Zach, crawling from under a loom "they do spells, aye, but we need summat as does practical work."

"Like Green Man does fer t'farms?" Sarah looked up from under another loom. "They say he can mek crops ripen overneet when t'weather's bin bad."

"Mebbe so," Zach replied, "but we're not in t'fields, we're in t'mill. And I dunt fancy losing a finger or freezin' me feet off afore I'm eleven like our Caleb."

"I dunt fancy fallen down dead either 'cos I'm too tired out. Me dad says we're going t'get even more t'do 'cos wool trade's getting' reet busy." Tom was the smallest amongst them, although at nine, one of the oldest.

"Well I reckon we need a brownie then," Edie said, sorting woollen bits from the dirt she'd swept up. "One o'them could help us do our jobs."

"She's right," Zach nodded, "we'll promise t'leave it in peace and give it a place to sleep."

"And ask no questions. They dunt like that." Sarah said, looking at the others.

"Nor offer it any clothing', they dunt like that either. But it will want milk and honey." Tom raised an eyebrow. "We all agreed then?" Everyone nodded. "Reet, we all 'ave to wish as 'ard as we can, and see what 'appens."

III

For several days they wished, looking around the mill expectantly each day when they arrived, hoping that jobs would have been done. Then one morning, just as they were losing hope, a small, wizened, brown figure with shaggy hair, wearing torn trousers whizzed past, invisible to any eyes but their own. Brownies you see, are shape-shifters. When anyone else looked up, the brownie became a cat slinking by, a bird, a fly.

The children were so happy but knew they had to keep doing their jobs so that the manager and Mr Sykes, the owner wouldn't get suspicious. Edie moved around sweeping floors which needed little sweeping; Zach and Sarah scavenged under the looms for the few bits of wool that were there; Tom got in the tubs to full the cloth which was done in record time. They shared their secret with the other children, all who promised to keep it and never to speak to the brownie.

For years everything went well. They didn't have to work so hard for their wages and the owner was pleased with his profit. As the children got older, new ones took their place, leaving the brownie in peace and milk and honey each night.

But one holiday, unusually, Mr Sykes toured the mill. Wandering around, he heard the noise of looms weaving cloth.

"Who on earth is here on a day off?" Wondering aloud, he walked into the fulling rooms where tubs were full of cloth, then into the sorting area, which was spick and span, the floor empty of even one strand of wool. Looking out, he exclaimed, "Am I going daft?" as he espied fulled cloth stretched out in the tenterfield.

Laughter from outside had him marching quickly to the door. Looking out, he could see some youths and children playing in the beck. "So, they're the ones!" he said to himself. "Strange thing to do on a day off! Hope they don't expect a bonus."

As he stepped over the threshold, out of the corner of his eye, he caught sight of a small, brown gnarled man dart past him with a pile of folded cloth in his arms. Startled, Mr Sykes shouted, "Who are you? What are you doing with my cloth?"

Turning, the brownie opened his mouth, making an ear-piercing howl which sent forth a foul breath, covering the owner, making him cough and splutter.

Outside the children and teenagers heard the howl and knew what it meant. They ran quickly into the mill, their hearts sinking as they saw the brownie shape-shift into the ugliest boggart they could imagine.

Its hair grew even longer, its legs shortened, teeth and nails grew until they curled inwards, its eyes glittered with evil. Howling once more it left a horrible stench behind as it disappeared into thin air.

IV

"That's it then," Tom said, "it'll all be disaster now."

Mr Sykes, a little in shock, turned to Tom. "What's tha mean? What'll be disaster? And what," he pointed to where the boggart had been, "was THAT?"

"He means everything'll go wrong," Sarah said.

"That were a boggart," added Zach.

"You shouldn't 'ave asked his name," Edie chipped in, "he were a reet good brownie." She started to cry.

"I've no idea what you're on about," the owner angrily declared. "Brownies, boggarts! No such thing. You'll be tellin' me next it's not you who's been workin' 'ere today. Circus trick that were, t'distract me from punishing you."

The youngsters, now in their teens, shook their heads sadly. Zach spoke for them all.

"Nay sir, 'twas a boggart alreet. They're as real as you or I. A brownie, once asked its name turns into a boggart and it'll plague you forever." Turning to the others, and to the children who were peeking in through the door, Zach continued, "Best be on t'lookout for another place, we won't be 'ere long."

"Now what does that mean?" spluttered Mr Sykes. "Old wives tales, that's what you're talking. We're in t'age o'science. Daft talk. Anyroad, I expect you to be back 'ere in t'morning and business as usual."

Striding out up the hill to his carriage, Mr Sykes didn't see the boggart following him or when it clambered into a box on the back or when it waved at the unhappy children.

V

From that day, as the youngsters had predicted, everything went wrong. The waterwheel at the mill kept stopping from stones that weighted it down; threads on the looms constantly snapped and each time the children pieced them together, they broke elsewhere; tubs of fulling cracked or suddenly overturned (luckily with no one in them); cloth stretched in the tenterfields was found up trees, in the river, or covered with animal droppings.

At first Mr Sykes blamed his workers. But the manager swore it couldn't be them.

"Me and t'overseer niver let 'em out of our sight, sir," he said. "They niver have t'opportunity."

As the problems carried on and got worse, the owner spent a week watching at the mill and saw for himself his workers were blameless.

He didn't know what to do. He'd been busy with orders from customers, but now when orders went out, there were complaints. The cloth was spoiled when it arrived, it had holes, it wasn't washed, it had shrunk or in some cases, it never arrived.

And it wasn't just at the mill that he had problems. At home, his wife and servants were at the end of their tether. Crockery was smashed almost daily, food rotted as soon as it was bought, fires and candles refused to light and bed covers were pulled off by unseen hands during the night.

Often, as they were walking from one room to another, servants would feel a pinch or a nip. The hound growled at empty corners of the room, horses whinnied and kicked in the stables for nights on end and visitors found their pockets had been picked.

The servants, fed up, began to leave. Workers had to be sacked because orders fell and eventually Mr Sykes's wife issued an ultimatum.

"I am leaving this place. I cannot stand this persecution any more. Anyone would think we were plagued by a boggart! We can leave and set up again elsewhere but only if you sell the mill."

The owner had said nothing about the boggart and he knew no one would buy a mill that wasn't prospering. So he closed it after selling all the looms and equipment and left the house and cottages empty.

On the day they were leaving, carriage and carts piled high with household goods, Tom, Sarah, Zach and Edie waited in the lane to watch the owner and his family pass by.

"We told him, but he dint listen." Zach sat on the wall, swinging his legs.

"I dunt know why folk dunt believe in 'em," Sarah said, plaiting some grasses. "There's a brownie or a boggart in every one of t'becks hereabouts me dad says."

"Aye, and this one's not bin as nasty as some," added Edie. "'Ey up, ere's Mr Sykes now."

Rumbling towards them was a carriage, the owner sitting on the front, his wife inside whilst behind the remaining two servants sat on a cart pulled by two horses. Slowing as they reached the youngsters, Mr Sykes reined in.

"So you're really going, sir?" Tom asked.

"Aye lad. Off to start again wi' some o'them new machines. I reckon looms and t'waterwheel were just too old. Mill's been there for years, wrong place nowadays. Need new technology. Onwards and upwards."

With a click of the tongue, he set the horses on their way, followed by the cart. They travelled on without a backward glance. If they had looked, they might have seen the lid of a box open slightly and a brown wizened face with glittering eyes appear, cackling to the youngsters as it passed, "Onwards and upwards!"

The Ride of Death

I

Peddling furiously into the darkening dusk, street lights barely visible in the gloom, I prayed I'd get home before Mum got back from work.

It was all Darren's fault. As usual, things hadn't gone to plan. He was late because he'd slept in; then he got a puncture, which of course I had to fix because he'd got no kit. By the time we'd got to the street festival, all the circus workshops were filled and it was a two hour wait to have a go in a canoe. Which, of course, he insisted on waiting for.

Mum would skin me alive if I wasn't there when she got

back. We'd made a bargain: I could bike with Darren to the festival *only* if her tea was on the table when she got in. Which, of course, would have been easy peasy if the plan had worked.

But instead, here I was biking in the rush hour, which could be dangerous even when it was light, even when you were in a bike lane, although it seemed quieter than usual tonight. I could just see Darren's rear light in front of me, he was always better on hills than me.

I heard the Town Hall bell chime.

My heart sank at the sixth peal, which of course, meant Mum would be home wondering where her tea was. I began to groan then realised the bell was still chiming. Ten, eleven, twelve!

"Darren!' I called out. 'Darren!" There was no answer.

Suddenly from nowhere came two huge galloping black horses with foaming mouths, wild eyes, steaming bodies and furiously swishing tails, heading straight for me. Surprise made me swerve and fall off my bike onto the damp grass. My back thudded against a hard stone surface, winding me and taking my breath away.

II

The horses skidded to a halt beside me, clouds of hot breath issuing from their quivering nostrils. Trembling, I tried to shout for Darren but only a pitiful squeak came out. As I lay there, stupified, I saw that something was emerging from the gloom, something that was attached to the horses. Slowly, the shape of an old-fashioned carriage appeared glowing eerily, like it was covered in luminous green paint.

It was a carriage, but not as big or decorated as the one we'd seen on the school trip to the Industrial Museum. Wooden wheels with an iron trim, a door with a window and a front seat for the driver. Not that there was a driver.

I didn't know what to think. Was Darren having a joke? Had I bumped my head when I fell and was hallucinating? I could feel my bike and that was real. And where *was* Darren? I tried to shout again. This time my squeak was louder but wobbly, betraying the fear that I was beginning to feel.

"Darren! Help!"

As I shouted, the carriage's gleam brightened, the horses shook their heads, pawed the ground and the door opened silently. A ghostly, gravelly voice announced, "Your carriage awaits you!"

Above me, I heard a noise. Looking up, I saw Darren's foot appear over my head, as he stretched it out to step into the carriage. I recognised his trainer with its frayed lace. Reaching out, I grabbed his foot.

"You're not having him!" I yelled, holding on as the foot disappeared inside.

Darren's body moved into the green glow as he stepped out from the gloom and off the mounting block I'd fallen against. His momentum dragged me forward.

I let go of his foot with my left hand and grasped it with my right one. Wrapping my left arm around his leg I tried to pull him back. He was very strong for such a small wiry boy. The whole of my body weight had no impact as he passed into the carriage. Once his feet were over the threshold, it began to move.

"No!" I screamed, half in and half out of the spectral vehicle.

My cry was drowned out by sinister laughter echoing around the interior.

III

I was being dragged along and as the horses' pace increased, I knew I had to either get inside with Darren or loosen my hold and drop before my feet were in shreds. But Darren was my best friend. Someone who listened to my woes and never judged me. He left me alone or tried to make me laugh when I was mardy. And he didn't care that he was made fun of because his best friend was a *'lumpy specky four-eyed'* girl.

I struggled to get my feet on the running board, shouting at Darren, asking for help. There was no sound or movement from him. I slid my right hand from his foot to the door-frame to get a grip, still holding onto his leg with my left. The door kept whacking me as the horses cantered forward. It felt like a piece of cloth, although I could see it was made of wood. Hauling myself inwards, using Darren's leg to pull against, I fell onto the floor, puffing, panting and petrified.

Sitting up, I looked at my friend. He was as stiff and still as a statue. When I touched him he was as cold as marble. His skin had an unearthly colour as if all the blood had been drained from him. I shook him, shouted at him, even slapped him. Nothing made a difference.

In despair, I sat next to him on the hard wooden, seat wondering what to do, how to get out of this nightmare. Which of course, was getting worse. Looking around I saw that the walls of the carriage were transparent. Darren and I seemed to be floating on the seat with the road whizzing past below our feet. I began to feel dizzy and gripped the seat with my hands, willing myself not to fall.

"Darren," I whispered to the silent stone-faced boy next to me, "we must get out of this. Something very bad is going to happen, I can feel it. Something much worse than this."

The hairs on the back of my neck bristled as demonic laughter echoed around us again.

It was then I realised that we were no longer on any road that I knew; there were no cars, houses or lights. Only the night sky and the glow from the carriage illuminated the fields flashing past. We rattled over a cobbled road and I almost toppled from my seat. Strangely, none of the erratic swaying which had me gripping the seat moved Darren at all. He simply sat there, fixed in position, staring ahead vacantly.

I screamed, as wet, slimy things slapped against my face

almost knocking off my glasses, blurring my vision even more.

IV

We'd entered a wood or forest. The wet slimy things were leaves. I could hear them slap Darren too, which told me we were on a very narrow track. I could hardly see anything in front of us. My bowels constricted as I sensed an evil presence beginning to fill the carriage.

Trying to clean the slime from my glasses, whilst still holding on, I was aware of a growing stench, like rotting meat. The horses' galloping became manic, sparks flying from their hooves as they hit the stones on the uneven ground. I was thrown around, hitting the sides of the carriage. Several times I fell against Darren but he was immovable.

The stench filled the carriage, I could almost taste it. My stomach heaved in revolt and I had to cover my mouth. Under the sound of the rushing wheels and hooves the sinister laughter began again, this time continuing, not stopping as before.

Up ahead I could make out a bit of a clearing, where trees

weren't so close to the track. I wondered whether, if I used all my strength, I'd be able to push Darren out there and jump after him. As this idea went through my head, the laughter got louder as if mocking my thought. Tears pricked my eyes and the laughter increased in volume.

We came to the clearing, where a watery moon showed a figure on the front seat. A figure in a ragged, torn cloak wearing a battered hat pulled down tightly about the ears. A hand holding a crop flashed above its head before whipping the horses into more of a frenzy. A hand where the flesh was hanging off in threads, where the bone showed through.

Hearing my scream, the figure turned. It was grotesque. There was only half a face, its flesh torn in shreds, an eyeball hanging from a thread. As I stared, horrified, the horses plunged down an incline, their hooves slipping under them, the carriage rocking dangerously. Seeing my panic and revulsion, the figure grinned horribly, pointed to Darren, then laughed hysterically, "Your carriage awaits you!"

Wanting to vomit at the sight and smell of this 'thing', I knew I had to keep strong. It was clear that we were heading to our deaths, that this ghoul was determined to to take Darren for his own and to smash us to pieces so that I died too. The thought of this scared me more than the nightmare we were in.

V

Suddenly the carriage rounded a corner on two wheels and for the first time, Darren was tossed from the corner he'd been fixed in, falling on me and pinning me to the floor. I closed my eyes because I could see the track below me zooming past. Struggling underneath him, pushing to free my arms, I heard myself shouting at him to move, heard the tears in my voice.

"Wha's matter Chel?" came Darren's voice in my ear.

"Darren! You're awake!" I exclaimed.

Darren shuffled until he was sitting on the floor. He frowned as he looked at me, rubbing his eyes.

"Wha's happening?" he asked sleepily. "Where's the bikes?"

The carriage lurched again, rolling us across the floor.

"Wha's that?" Darren's eyes were now fully open.

"No time to tell you," I declared. "You have to trust me and do what I say." Which of course, was the reverse of what usually happened, so I wasn't sure he'd go along with the plan that I'd begun to form.

"Chel. The ground is rushing away under my feet." Darren was staring at the floor. "How can that be? Where -?"

A great peal of cackling laughter cut through what he was going to say and looking up, he caught site of the ghoulish driver. Before Darren could question me, I grabbed his shirt, pulled him to me and whispered urgently into his ear.

"And don't let your fear show," I finished. "I think the 'thing' feeds off it and gets stronger when it can see you're scared."

Darren nodded his agreement and we sat there as the carriage careered down the hill, holding onto each other for strength, listening to the monotonous laughter. We were silent, waiting for a change of direction from the horses.

"Now!" I shouted as we rounded another corner.

We threw ourselves to the right wall of the carriage as it lurched onto two wheels, making it rock so hard that the wheels slipped and the carriage overturned. It smashed down onto the track, pulling the horses down with it. I'd told Darren to grab hold of the carriage door on the other side as soon as the carriage began to tip, so that we wouldn't be smashed too.

We lurched through the open the door, scrambling out into the night as fast as we could. Darren fell, bashing his ankle on the wheel-axle and groaned with pain. A frenzied cry spread through the trees, freezing my blood. A 'whoosh' sounded very close to us as the ghoul's whip lashed the carriage door.

"Come on Darren," I urged, grabbing his hand, "we've got to get away from here." I yanked him up and set off, pulling him after me.

"Painful Chel," he whimpered. "Can't run. You go." His hand began to slip from mine. There was no way I was letting him stay. I knew he'd be dead if I did.

I slapped him, hard.

"Chel!" he yelled, eyes wide in amazement. Above his head, I saw the whip descending and managed to push him out of the way before it cut his face.

"You are coming with me," I hissed, "and you're coming now before that 'thing' gets hold of you!"

Darren's eyes widened further, his mouth opening to shout something and I knew it wasn't going to be good.

VI

A bony hand with tendrils of flesh clamped my neck slowly choking me, the rotting stench filling my nose. I tried to pull the ghoul off me, but the pressure increased until I saw spots dancing in front of my eyes. I couldn't breathe. The demonic laugher filled my head. I was going to die.

Dimly aware of the hand slackening, I fell down in a heap, coughing and clutching my neck. Behind me, Darren was screaming, "Leave her alone! Leave her alone!" over and over. The demonic laughter stopped. The noise of the thrashing horses stopped.

Instead, I heard sobbing. Getting up, I turned to see Darren in a heap, his body shaking. I'd never seen him cry, not even when he was being bullied at school. I went over and put my arms round him.

"It's OK," I whispered, my throat hurting as I spoke. At Darren's feet was a ragged, torn cloak and a battered hat. No sign of a carriage, horses or a narrow track through trees. We were by the mounting block, bikes laying on the grass, dim street lights glowing in the gloom.

"What happened?" I managed to croak.

"He was choking you," Darren's voice wobbled. "Your eyes were bulging. I could hear you gasping. I didn't know what to do." His voice rose. "I found the penknife in my pocket and I just ran at him – it – and plunged the penknife in his eye again and again." He shuddered. "It tried to grab me but every time I plunged, it got weaker and faded, like the carriage and horses, until there was nothing there."

Darren mumbled, "What was it Chel? What did it want?"

I shook my head. "I don't know. I don't want to know. I want to forget as quick as I can. I don't want to talk about it again."

Darren nodded. "Me neither. But if you hadn't been with me -," I stopped him.

"We're quits," I said, "so let's leave it there."

We raised our heads at the chiming of the Town Hall bell. Listening closely, we heard it chime five times, then no more. We looked at each other in wonder.

"Back in time to keep your bargain," Darren smiled weakly, getting on his bike. "Last one back's a sissy!" he shouted, setting off.

Which, of course I was.

Playing in the Park

Walking at midnight in Bradford Town
I saw a clutch of Kings frolic and clown,
Paddling around in the ancient stream
Flicking water at an illustrious Queen.

"It's boring," they said, "being still all day,
When over this land we once held sway.
From civil war ghosts and a ravaging boar,
We're featured often in this town's folklore.

People knew of us, they were awed by our deeds
Recognising the strengths of one who leads.
Once upon a time we stood here proud
Knowing we attracted an admiring crowd.

Now we're so tired of being on view
Rarely noticed and looked at by so few.
So each evening at midnight we forget rival claims
Stepping down to indulge in a few friendly games."

I saw Anne and a Henry playing piggy-in-the-middle,
Charles I and James II plinking on a fiddle.
Edward III chased John through the waters
While Henry VIII danced galliards with his daughters.

"We missed out," said Mary, "when I was a maid,
So we catch up on memories before they fade."
William whooped, "Hide and seek! You're on Lizzie."
First one caught is a right royal sissy!"

They ran hither and thither around City Park,
Peeping out when hidden from behind silver bark.
Tag, marbles, hopscotch, played with a gleeful yell
By all except, of course, party-pooping Cromwell.

Through the night they continued, until with a yawn
They climbed to their perches at the hint of dawn.
A strange tale I know, about the town's fine hall,
But believe me, every night, those statues have a ball.

Heads It Is

I

I lost my head in one of the last battles when invaders from Olicana came storming over the hills, along the river bed and up through the forest to our settlements in the clearings across the valley.

I was the powerful leader of my tribe, revered and courted by Brigantian Kings and Queens for my counsel and magic as well as my warrior skills. Yes, it's true, our tribes collected the heads of those we killed in battle but not to gloat about how many we'd killed as the Romans said. No! It was make sure their souls were taken care of, for we believed the soul of a person lives in their head. To have your soul escape because a wild animal has eaten your face or brains was the worst thing we could think of.

Not that the Romans saw it this way. Barbaric is what they called it, saying we pinned the heads to our horses' manes or to doors. Julius Caesar himself told people this. All lies to make us look bloodthirsty and less civilised than they. But we had Queens who ruled and our women had their say as much as the men, unlike the invaders.

II

When our scout returned to tell us the Romans were on the move, we laid physical and magical traps. At the last full moon we'd slaughtered cattle and laid them in pits covered with hawthorn branches. We chanted around the oaks, ancient even then, asking forgiveness for cutting them to make spikes to sink into the ground as a defensive boundary.

Wearing my circlet of holly I'd walked the perimeter of

our settlement beating the ground with rowan, the womenfolk squashing the berries underfoot, leaving a trail as red as the blood our enemies would spill. Supping a fermented potion of herbs and berries, I sweated alone in my hut, opening my mind and soul for guidance.

We were betrayed. Just as Cartimandua had handed our rebel leader Caratacus to the Romans some years before, then taken on their ways, one of our tribe was seduced by their promises of wealth. He'd sneaked away after our preparations and given the details to the cohort's leader.

They came creeping through the alder and hazel, killing the sentries silently where they stood guard, unsuspecting that the friendly greeting they exchanged with the traitor was their death sentence.

We fought hard, the women as well as the men. Our spears, axes and arrows forged in the charcoal heat by skilled workers had served us well in many skirmishes with hostile tribes. But the betrayal meant the Romans were stronger in number and well-prepared.

As the chief and magician, I was their main target. I knew what they wanted – my head. To put on a pole to be mocked as they walked through their camp then left for the wolves to devour. I fought hard, the fermented potions giving me three times my usual strength as I slashed out with my sword. I took many men, well satisfied when I put an end to the traitor's life.

Around me the noise of cattle and horses stampeding, the squawking of headless chickens, the cries, shouts, curses and screams, the smell of burning as huts were fired – all gave my sword arm more power.

To protect me, the men and women created an arrow formation, throwing spears, thrusting with their swords and daggers, trying to drive the Olicana legionnaires onto the spikes or down to the river where the water was dangerously deep with a strong undertow.

Eventually the enemy's superior weaponry won over ours. Their swords were short, light and easier to handle than our heavy weapons; they were quick with their sharp daggers, their spears penetrating our wooden shields and their armour gave them advantage over our unprotected heads and bodies.

As a rosy, blue-tinted dusk painted the sky, I felt a sharp stabbing pain at the back of my neck, heard a roar of victory from the enemy and one of despair from my tribe.

My eyes sought each of my friends as my head soared

above them, bidding them a farewell from this physical world. Romans ran, jostling each other, cursing and fighting to be the one to catch my head as it fell.

In this they were thwarted. It landed in a hole at the foot of an ancient oak, a large hollow created by boars digging for acorns and truffles. Swiftly, with a slight moan, the tree moved its roots to cover me whilst a soft breeze blew leaves into a mound over them.

Before I was hidden, I caught the eye of young Anya, who was halfway up the tree, sheltering from the carnage below. She sat as still as a bird roosting for the night, her brown dress and cloak hiding her well. Bright blue eyes caught my blink and she smiled her understanding.

III

Angry at not having my head as a trophy to parade around Olicana and claim a reward from their camp prefect, the cohort took their fury out on my people. Many died, others were taken as slaves for hard labour and domestic duties.

But some of the children, like Anya, had managed to hide in the trees watching the battle and slaughter, only venturing forth when they were certain the enemy had finally departed.

Children were taught our ways from being babes, so they knew our rites of the dead. Between them they honoured their families as best they could, dragging wives to be with husbands, placing babes in mothers' arms. Huts had been set alight so no possessions could be collected to help the dead on their journey, but the children gathered weapons and shields not carried away by the departing Romans.

Weapons were laid with the warriors and as a hole couldn't be dug in which to lay them, they were covered with the shields. Boughs of hawthorn, rowan and holly were laid on top, all powerful protectors from evil and witchcraft. Together the children prayed to the Gods for the souls of their family and friends for a safe journey to the next world. When this was complete Anya approached the tree she'd sheltered in and chanted:

Ancient oak whose acorns make our daily bread,
Who gives them freely so our boars are fed,
Whose boughs have moaned and bled
To protect us, and who watches over our dead.
I ask you to give up the one who led,
So I may create a shrine for the head.

The mound of leaves swirled and eddied upward uncovering the tree's roots. Over these she sprinkled blood from one of the slaughtered chickens. Soft moans were heard as the roots moved, revealing my head and my gold torque. My eyes locked with Anya; my thoughts filled her mind as I told her which herbs to collect so that we could make powerful magic against the invaders.

Around us the trees shook, the wolves howled and through parted clouds the moon shone. Smiling, Anya picked me up, gently cleaning the blood from my face, taking the gold torque from my neck. She placed me and the torque in a bag which she slung over her shoulder.

Returning to the village, all was silence. No children or livestock remained, only the mound of sacred boughs covering our dead. The children who escaped took their chances in the woods and forests, evading capture at all costs.

We walked, Anya and I to the Spring of the Seven Sacred Saplings. Under the elder, we invoked the guardian dryad Hylde-Moer and asked her permission to use bark and berries. These would be mixed with the leaves of the Sacred Saplings to create a curse on our enemy. The tree dipped its branches for Anya to collect what she needed whilst bark unpeeled from the trunk.

Scraping at the ground, Anya made a hollow into which she placed the bark, berries, leaves from the Sacred Saplings and the herbs she'd collected. Sparks created with her flint fell on the kindling, becoming flames as she blew. Once the fire took hold, she held my head, letting blood drip from my neck onto the flames, intoning:

> *Our enemies shall rue the day*
> *When their feet trod our way.*
> *Not one who took a life*
> *By the new moon will be alive.*
> *We place curse on you who kill*
> *This is our goddess's will.*

A crack of thunder and a bolt of lightening ripped through the night. The Goddess had spoken.

IV

Anya made a bed of leaves, laid down and immediately

fell asleep. I watched over her, knowing she would be safe. The wolves of the forest never visited after the Goddess had spoken.

On the morrow Anya carried me to a fissure in the rock from which water emerged, ran into the beck then flowed down the valley to the sea. She placed my head in the fissure. The life-giving water would feed my soul, enriching its powers to reach out to my people and give them hope.

Next, she took some flints from her bag and began to chip away at the rock in the fissure to create an image of my face. The carving would show my tribe where to find me to seek guidance. My soul would be held in my image should my skull disappear.

She didn't stop until she was done, drinking the sweet water, nibbling on nuts and berries as the sun rose and set three times. When she had finished Anya slept for two days above me in the grove of the Sacred Saplings, missing the new moon. I spoke softly to her mind about the future and how our world was changing forever, how soon we would be gone and only echoes of us would remain.

On the fifth day, one of the youths who had been taken with the Romans came straggling back to our ravaged settlement. Anya had seen him wading across the river using the safe crossing known only to us. He was almost naked, with welts across his back from beatings, his feet bleeding from sharps stones. Anya took his hand as he reached the bank and led him to the grove, sitting him by the fire to warm in her brown cloak. He wolfed down some fish she'd caught earlier.

When he had stopped shivering, he told her of the massacre that had happened on the night of the new moon. After being beaten, starved and pelted with rotten food by a vicious overseer, the men had been marched out to dig new earthworks several miles north to a hill surrounded by a wooded valley.

Guarding them were all the soldiers who had ambushed us, who took great delight in mocking the chained men, taunting about their weak Gods, hurling abuse and whipping the men whilst they worked. Unbeknown to the Romans, another local Brigante tribe had been watching them for the past few months waiting for a time to mount a surprise attack.

On the day of the new moon, the Romans were pushing our men hard to break rock. The overseer was particularly brutal that day having been reprimanded by the cohort leader for not meeting his targets. As night fell and the exhausted men got in line for the tramp across the hills, frenzied battle cries filled the air as blue-faced men and women came hurtling out of the woods.

The Romans were unprepared. They fought bravely but the Brigantian numbers overwhelmed them, killing each and every one. Collecting Roman weaponry for future skirmishes, the victors released our men from chains and took them into their own community, despite previous quarrels between our tribes.

Falling silent, the boy took a drink. Anya asked about the women and girls. They had become slaves he told her, close guarded. Boys too, doing hard work were whipped like the men. When news of the massacre was brought, all the slaves were punished severely. Many died from their beatings.

He'd managed to hide in a large amphora being taken to Eboracum to be re-filled. When the driver of the convoy stopped for a call of nature, the boy had slipped away into the cover of some trees, waiting till nightfall to find his way back. Now he was unsure what to do, with no family, no home and no tribe. Anya told him to sleep, saying guidance would be given in the morning.

After dawn broke, Anya showed him my shrine and invited him to go with her to take the news of my resting place North through the communities subdued by Roman rule. They took my torque and together travelled far and wide.

Most of the native tribes carried on as before tilling the land, raising livestock. Slowly, through marriage between our tribes and the invaders, some Brigantines took on Roman ways.

Those who didn't, came to my shrine pay homage to their kith and kin, to celebrate our past victories, our way of life and to remember the old ways. Once they were dead, I was forgotten, even though my powers still pulsed through the spring and my wisdom was there for any who could hear.

V

It took thousands of years to be discovered. I was brought into the light as centuries of silt was dug away. I felt a ray of sun on my face, the kiss of a breeze and the smell of the trees around me. Holly, oak, rowan, hawthorn. How how long I'd waited! My soul sang.

A strong jet of water blasted it into my sightless eyes and around the fissure, shifting the silt. The shaft of light warming me increased, bathing my whole face. A few moments later the darkness was gone and I was once again amongst the living, though the two specimens before me neither looked nor sounded like warriors. Their pasty skin, strange garb and puny stature would have been no match for me. Their faces showed their surprise at finding my skull.

The voices babbled. It wasn't a language I knew though I could tell they were arguing. I stared past the pair to the trees in my grove. The original Seven Sacred Saplings were gone but others now sprouted. Walls of the huts that once housed my people were buried deep in the humus of the rotting trees waiting to be unearthed.

Over time my skull had become attached to the fissure. The men, like Anya with her flints, slowly and gently with very small daggers, chipped away until they could get me out without breaking me.

Laying me in soft bag and then a box that once again blocked out the daylight, they carried me far from my home. But my face is still there, carved into the rock that now holds my soul.

Anyone who can read the signs can find me. If they place their hand inside the fissure under the water and rub it across the rock, they will feel me and my power, ready when the time is right to defend my people once more.

Theatrical Spirits

I

"Will you tell that girl to stop giggling! We can't hear what you're singing!"

The theatre technician's voice boomed over the tannoy, interrupting the All Stars Drama Academy's rehearsal for their annual extravaganza. To make sure everything went smoothly on the night, the techs were plotting the music, light and sound cues.

"What girl?" Tyler asked, looking at the others. None of them were giggling. Along with Charmaine, Max, Shannon and Shaz, he was rehearsing their Bollywood song and dance spoof.

"Are there any girls backstage?" Mrs Jennings, their drama teacher shouted. "If there are, please shut UP!"

"Miss, there's no-one backstage," Shaz said. "They've all gone for lunch while we practise. They said they wouldn't be back till two."

"Good! Then we can get on with it." Mrs Jennings turned and gave a thumbs-up to the tech box, waiting for the red light so the dancers could continue.

"And from the top! 3, 2, 1!"

Music blasted out from the speakers into the auditorium, empty except for the children. Shaz began to sing as the others started their routine, feet tapping, hands twirling, bodies circling, costumes winking and glittering in the lights. Less than two minutes in, the tannoy blared again.

"Will that girl STOP giggling! We'll never get the cues down at this rate!"

Everything stopped. Silence fell. Nothing could be heard except the children's breathing. Everyone listened hard, frowns on their faces. Nothing!

Mrs Jennings picked up a voice mic, saying, "There's

absolutely no sound here." She turned again to the tech box.

"There must be!" a tetchy voice announced. "We can hear it in the cans!"

Exasperated, Mrs Jennings shook her head. The youngsters glanced at each other, shrugging, facial expressions indicating they had no idea what was going on.

"Max, Shannon," Mrs Jennings pointed, "go backstage and check there's no-one messing about. Charmaine and Tyler, go to the Green Room to see if anyone has smuggled a mic down there. Shazia, you check front of house. If I find that any of the cast are mucking about, they're out of this show."

II

Happily, Shaz set off for the foyer. It meant that she could nip to the loo, something she'd wanted to do for ages but Mrs Jennings was very strict when rehearsing.

She met no-one on her way downstairs, not even the theatre manager who always seemed to be scurrying somewhere. It was very quiet. She thought about how different the theatre was when a show was on, full of noise and chatter, a magical place. Not empty and silent like now.

Coming out of the loo, Shaz found one of the theatre cats sitting staring at the entrance to the bar. Rubbing her fingers together, Shaz knelt down calling "Ch, ch, ch." Usually the cat came straight away wanting to be petted and stroked. Not today. Back straight, eyes fixed unwaveringly on the entrance, ears flicking to and fro, it ignored her outstretched hand.

Shaz wondered what it was looking at, she could see nothing. Suddenly the cat hissed, fur spiked on its back, ears flattened, its tail bushed out and it rose on four paws, ready to pounce.

Coming through the entrance was a man in a top hat, black cloak, white gloves and shiny buttoned shoes. Spitting as the man neared, the cat gave a stricken yowl before bolting up the stairs. "Cats are strange things!" Shaz thought watching it disappear. She turned her gaze back to the man.

"Great costume," she said. There was no reply. A cold sensation went through Shaz as he passed her, so cold that she shivered, feeling goosebumps on her arms. Then she realised that there were no footsteps. The man seemed to be gliding on air.

Wary, her eyes followed his passage across the foyer. She thought he was going to climb the stairs to the auditorium. Instead he headed to the Green Room entrance. Her heart almost stopped as she watched him disappear straight through the closed and locked door.

For a few moments she was rooted to the spot. Then, like the cat, she bolted up the stairs shouting, "Mrs Jennings! Mrs Jennings!"

III

Meanwhile, Max and Shannon had carried out a thorough search backstage, making sure there was no-one up in the fly tower. Coming back, Max looked for their teacher.

"Mrs Jennings!" Shannon called, "Shaz was right. There's no-one there."

There was no reply. Max called too, but still no answer. It was hard to see if anyone was out front because the stage lights were so bright.

"Maybe she's on the phone," Max said. "Let's find her and tell her."

They jumped down into the stalls, searching the seats with

their eyes.

"She doesn't seem to be here," Shannon said. "Maybe she's gone to talk to the techs."

"Isn't that her in the circle?" Pointing, Max called again. "Mrs Jennings, we've checked backstage and it's empty. Can we go and get a drink?"

Shannon looked to where Max pointed. She could see a female sitting in the middle of a row, but she didn't look like Mrs Jennings. This one was wearing a high-collared blouse with a brooch at the neck, a grey jacket and her hair was in a big bun. Her face was hard to see in the gloom.

"It's not Mrs Jennings Max. But she might know where she is."

"Excuse me," Max piped up, "Have you seen our teacher, Mrs Jennings?"

The woman's head lowered slightly. A gloved hand reached forward, a finger beckoning them.

"Why can't she just say yes or no?" Max grumbled, "instead of calling us to the Circle."

As Max turned to go, Shannon saw the woman stand. She was wearing a grey two-piece suit, a small hat perched on the back of her bun with a veil covering her face.

"Great costume," Shannon said to herself. Fumbling in her pocket, she pulled out her mobile, zoomed in the camera and took a picture. The flash lit the woman's face, making Shannon's eyes widen. Scrolling quickly to the image, it proved what she thought she'd seen.

"Max! Don't go up there!" Shouting, Shannon scrambled after him, trying to catch up.

"What d'you mean?" Max's voice echoed down the stairwell.

Stumbling up the steps, Shannon cried, "Don't! Don't go near her!"

"Why not?"

Shannon heard Max open the Circle door and ran as fast as she could. Slipping through the opening before the door closed, she managed to grasp Max's sleeve.

As they stopped at the end of he row, the woman turned her head, her finger beckoning them again.

"See, she wants to tell us something." Max started forward but Shannon grabbed him round the waist, holding him tightly.

"No! You can't!" she shouted.

"What? Why?" Max spluttered, struggling against her.

"Because she's got no face!"

"No face?" Max turned his head to stare at Shannon.

"No face!" she repeated.

A sound made them start and look round. The woman had moved closer. Holding their breath, the children watched as the woman raised her veil revealing a head that had no facial features. The children's scream resounded around the auditorium.

IV

On their way down to the Green Room, Tyler and Charmaine were swapping stories about the theatre as both their dads had been involved with it.

"At least I've heard of that film," Tyler said, replying to Charmaine. "My dad said lots of famous actors started out here, but when he showed me his pictures, I didn't know any of them. They were ancient."

"They'll be from back in the day," Charmaine responded. "It's an old place. You can tell that from all these back stairs and the shape of the building *and* that 'old' smell."

"Yea, there's definitely a smell," Tyler agreed. "And that

picture shows what I mean. How old is that?"

They stopped in front of a sepia photograph showing a woman in a white lacy dress, a glittering tiara atop her ringlets from which a white veil hung. She stood next to a coffin that had a vase of white lilies on it.

"Looks Victorian," Tyler said.

"Great costume," Charmaine said, before peering at the writing at the bottom of the picture. "Bride of Dracula, 1963," she read. "Wrong! Still ages ago though."

They continued down, meeting no one. "Strange we can't hear anyone Tyler. The chaperones are supposed to stay. Urgh, there's spiders' webs all over."

Tyler didn't like spiders, so his pace increased, making him stumble. "The walls are dead clammy too," he wiped his hand on his pantaloons. "Probably 'cos were so far down. Hang on! What's that noise?"

"What noise?"

"That one."

A wavering voice could be heard nearby. As the children listened, music drifted along the corridor from the Green Room door.

"Someone rehearsing," Charmaine said. "Let's see if

they're the one with the mic."

Walking forward, Tyler opened the door, sniffing. "The smell's stronger here. And that's very strange music."

Although it was soft, it sounded off-key, as did the oddly wavering voice.

"Well, they're not rehearsing anything from our show, that's for sure." Charmaine covered her ears. "It's weird."

Tyler stuck his head in Dressing Room 1 and 2 while Charmaine headed for 3. The light flickered in the corridor, throwing shadows across the walls. Suddenly there was a shriek from Charmaine.

"What's the matter Char?" Tyler ran out to find her laughing.

"Nothing. I saw myself in the mirror at the end. I forgot it was there. I thought it was a spook!"

Tyler rolled his eyes. Girls!

"There's no-one in either 1 or 2 and no mics that I can find," he told her. "That leaves 3, which is where my rucksack is, containing bags of crisps!"

Music and voice increased in volume as the youngsters neared the doorway. "There's that smell again." Charmaine sniffed. "It's a flowery sort of perfume."

"Must be rotting flowers then." Tyler wrinkled his nose in disgust. Slipping into the room, he saw it was empty. "Where's the music and voice coming from?" he asked his companion.

"Maybe someone's left an ipod playing," she suggested from behind him. "Where's your bag, I'm starvenous."

Tyler reached for a red rucksack under a table. "Salt and vinegar or cheese and onion?"

When Charmaine hadn't answered after a few moments, Tyler looked up from delving in his bag. Her mouth was agape as if in a silent scream, her face drained of colour, an image of fear stamped there.

"Char? You OK?" Tyler put his hand on her arm, which was as cold and clammy as the walls. "Char?" he repeated. She didn't move, just stared at the mirror behind him.

Slowly, Tyler twisted his head to look. In the mirror, a woman in white, softly singing in a wavering voice, holding rotting white lilies, stood next to a coffin. On top of this was a wind-up gramophone, from which the music came.

The children stood transfixed. When a hand reached forward, appearing through the mirror into the room, Tyler screamed, snapping Charmaine out of her trance. Grabbing his wrist, she ran from the room, pulling him behind her.

V

An argument was in full swing in the tech box whilst the children went searching.

"I can tell you there was no giggling from any of the dancers." Mrs Jennings was getting red in the face from her anger. They were on a tight deadline to get things polished before the show. What she didn't need right now were people playing games.

"And I can tell you that a girl was giggling the whole time you were on stage. I could hear her." Rick, adamant he was right, leaned against the sound desk, arms folded, hair messy from running his hands through it in frustration. He never liked working on children's shows, something always went wrong.

"We couldn't hear anything. It was totally silent. I've sent the youngsters to check out if any of the cast have been messing about but I can't see it. The chaperones are very strict and eagle-eyed." Mrs Jennings drummed her fingers.

"OK, let me prove it." Rick picked up a pair of cans from

next to the sound desk. "Here."

Taking them, the drama teacher lifted one to her ear. "Turn it on then," she said impatiently.

Rick flicked a switch and the desk lit up; reds, greens, blues indicating sound levels and cues. He moved a lever until a cue number showed. "See what you think."

Raising an eyebrow, Mrs Jennings listened to the sound in the cans. Rick smiled as he saw a frown develop on her forehead and her mouth form "What!?"

She could hear the recording of the last rehearsal they'd done. The music loud, Shaz's voice, dancers' shuffling; but a few seconds in, louder than all of that, was the sound of a girl giggling. A giggle that was almost out of control, like when something has made you laugh so much you're almost crying. The sound made the hairs on the back of the teacher's neck stand up.

Casting the cans on the table, Mrs Jennings exclaimed, "I just don't understand! We couldn't hear anything! Maybe you've got two cues together," the teacher suggested. "Recorded one over the other?"

Rick's sceptical look said what he thought of her suggestion. "Mrs Jennings, I've been doing this for many years. I *never* mix up cues or record one over another. That voice was as alive as the youngsters on the stage." He ran his hand through his hair again, messing it even more.

"I suspect what you do. It's someone in the cast. Maybe they're miffed that they didn't get a starring role."

Mrs Jennings nodded. It happened. Children could take things so personally and get really upset at not getting a role they wanted.

"OK," she said. "I'll go back to the auditorium and find out what the children have discovered. If I do find -,"

A blood-curdling scream penetrated through the half-open door, silencing Mrs Jennings. She and Rick exchanged glances. He was about to speak when another scream sounded, making them rush out of the tech box to the stairs.

VI

Thumping footsteps could be heard from various directions as Rick and Mrs Jennings arrived at the door to the stalls. They could hear several scared voices shouting "Mrs Jennings! Mrs Jennings!"

"Shazia? What's going on?"

A panting Shaz appeared on the downstairs landing, red-faced from climbing the stairs so fast. At the same time Max and Shannon, clinging to each other, faces white with fear careered down the Circle staircase towards the adults. Suddenly the stall doors flew open as Charmaine and Tyler burst through, almost knocking Mrs Jennings over.

The children jostled, trying to get their stories out, a babble of words erupting, loud, confused, running into each other and making no sense to the listeners.

"Whoa!" Rick shouted, his hands in the air. "Slow down. One at a time!"

His shout startled them. One red, two white and two ashen faces, each with fear in their eyes and shaking bodies stopped mid-flow.

"Calm down. Let's sit on the stage and you can tell us why you're all so agitated," Rick said holding the door open.

On stage, Mrs Jennings told them to put their Academy t-shirts on to get warm. She was feeling concerned, and confused. The day had certainly become strange.

Whispering, the boys and girls were huddled together. Max and Shannon avoided looking up at the Circle; Tyler and Charmaine kept turning their heads to check there was nothing at the top of the backstage steps and Shaz sat biting her nails.

Turning, Mrs Jennings was upset to see the children looking so stricken on what was supposed to be an exciting day. It had started out so well.

"Look everyone," she began, "I don't know what's been going on. It's probably some sort of joke, in very poor taste, and you shouldn't let it -"

She faltered as Shannon and Max whimpered and fear flickered on the faces in front of her. The stage lights dimmed, a strong smell of lilies swept over the stalls, then quiet giggling began.

"No!" Charmaine cried, cringing, putting her hands up as if to ward something off.

"You're not real. You're not real." Max chanted, hands over his ears.

"What the -!" Rick exclaimed as a white gloved hand stroked his face and lily petals drifted around him.

Mrs Jennings, feeling she was being watched, felt the hairs on the back of her neck raise again. Slowly turning her head, her eyes stared into a face of skin, devoid of any features.

Noiselessly, the man in the top hat appeared on stage making Shaz's bladder quiver, especially when he reached under his cloak and produced a white cat. The giggling increased in volume, other voices joining in. Wriggling, the cat yowled, spat, hissed, jumped out of the top-hatted man's hands and shot out of the auditorium at break-neck speed.

It had an immediate effect on the children.

"Follow that cat!" Max shouted, grabbing Shannon's hand, pulling her down the stage steps and heading for the door. Charmaine, Tyler and Shaz followed. They reached the open doorway and leapt down the stairs two at a time. Mrs Jennings and Rick ran after them. Giggling voices chased them down the stairwell, the volume increasing so much that it hurt their ears.

In the foyer, the children were frantically trying to unlock the door, rattling and kicking it in desperate frustration and anger. Rick pushed through them and tried to force the deadlock while the children continued kicking, hands over their ears.

From nowhere, a great whoosh of warm air blew Mrs Jennings into them. It became stronger and stronger until they found it hard to stand upright if they moved. Increasing in power, it blew the doors wide open and everyone into the street. They lay for a few minutes stunned, staring at the theatre entrance.

Mrs Jennings was the first to recover. "Is anyone hurt?" she asked, offering a hand to the youngsters to help them get up.

"Never mind that," said Rick, "let's get out of the road and into the cafe round the corner. We can check there in safety."

The youngsters began talking at once as they set off down the street, Rick in front and Mrs Jennings bringing up the rear. They'd just turned right into the main street when a huge explosion sounded behind them, causing the children to shriek and grab each other.

VII

"What the -!" Rick and Mrs Jennings exclaimed together.

Peeping around the corner, the group saw sheets of flame licking the sky from a hole in the theatre roof. Tiles and debris had smashed windows in the apartment building opposite. Residents were appearing, faces full of disbelief, voices loud with anxiety. Sirens could be heard in the distance, getting louder every moment.

"Miss," Shaz said shakily, "we could have been in there when that happened."

"We could have been fried!" Tyler exclaimed.

"Or blown to bits." Charmaine joined in.

"We could have joined those ghosts!" Shannon cried.

"You don't think," Max said slowly, "that they were frightening us so we'd leave?"

Eyebrow raised, Mrs Jennings looked at him questioningly.

"Well, maybe they knew what was going to happen," he explained, "and they were saving us by scaring us."

Mrs Jennings didn't know what to say. Before today she didn't believe in ghosts, the supernatural, spectres or any 'haunted' nonsense. Rick hadn't either, but the giggling girl, the feel of the glove on his face and the lilies were beginning to make him doubt.

"Maybe we'll never know," Max said, staring at the flames. "But it's true that because of them we're alive."

Shannon gasped. "My mobi!" Fumbling in her pocket, she went on, "I took a pic when we were searching."

Clicking 'photos' she scrolled to the last picture and gasped again. She passed the phone around, where everyone could see the image of the grey-suited woman. There were no blank face this time but a soft elderly one with smiling eyes.

A shiver passed through the group. Unconsciously, Max held his hands out to Shannon and Tyler, who did the same to Charmaine and Shaz. Mrs Jennings and Rick held a child's hand at either end of the line as three fire engines turned into the street followed by a police car.

Secret of the Sphinxes

I

Dusk was about to fall as the youngsters returned from school through the cemetery. Tombs, mausoleums and monuments lit by the lowering sun cast shadows on the promenade. Sitting at the base of the tall obelisk that gazed out over the city, they shared sweets and drinks, chatted about their day, played games on their phones and texted friends.

Facing west, the obelisk always had the last of the sun. So

it was only when they got up to go that the children realised how dark the rest of the cemetery had become.

"Let's get a move on," Fatima said, zipping her bag and glancing around. "It'll be proper dark by the time we get to the gates."

"Not scared are you?" Luca mocked, picking up his rucksack. "Nothing to be scared of. We walk through here every day."

"Yeh, but I know what she means," Sienna said, shrugging on her coat. "Look at those shadows. That angel lying there," she pointed to a tomb as they passed, "that could be a dead body."

Fatima shivered. "That's horrible!"

Luca laughed at them. "We can see the street lights down there and the cars! It's only four-thirty, not the middle of the night!" He laughed again. "Bet you can't catch me!"

Breaking into a run, he dodged around and between them, then disappeared into the gloom. They heard him racing down the steps.

"Luca!" the girls shouted, moving closer and linking arms as they hurried on. Around them, the shadows deepened, brambles and trees rustled as birds began to settle for the night. A squirrel loped across the path making the girls squeal, jump and laugh nervously at themselves. Granite and stone faces poked through thickets of rhododendron, white headstones glinted through the long grass. The hum of nearby roads could be heard but the cemetery itself was quiet.

Moving ever quicker, Sienna and Fatima jogged down the embankment steps. It was darker here amongst the tall monuments to the wealthy dead of the city's past. Both girls tripped on the uneven ground.

"I'll shine my phone," Sienna said pointing it along the path, "we'll be able to see better."

Coming down the next set of steps, Fatima tensed, whispering, "What's that?" They both listened intently and heard a low moaning, like someone in pain.

"If that's Luca playing games," Sienna fumed, "it's not funny!" Moving swiftly, she pulled Fatima with her onto the path below.

The moaning was louder here, off to their right. Shining their phones they peered through the headstones, seeing Luca with his back pressed against the door of a fancy tomb.

"Luca, what's up?" Fatima walked towards the grey

edifice, Sienna following. As they passed between the two statues in front of the tomb, Luca moaned again, "No! No!" His head shook from side to side, his eyes stared vacantly in front of him.

"If this is some sort of joke Luca Pavlovicz -," Sienna began but Fatima grabbed her arm. "Ow! Fatima, that hurts! Are you two in this joke together?" Sienna tried to prise her friend's fingers from her arm, but realised Fatima was whimpering.

"Sienna," Fatima gasped, "the statues are moving!"

II

Looking round, Sienna saw that the grey sphinxes at each side of them were vibrating, transforming, growing huge. The hybrid statues, with a woman's face and a lion's body had become living, breathing things with blazing topaz eyes and head-dresses of vivid blues and gold that glowed and shimmered.

It wasn't only the sphinxes creating the fear and confusion that surged through the children. Instead of the grey tomb behind Luca, there now stood a huge sandstone palace with doors of gold. A hot sun beat down, the smell of spices wafted around them and camels brayed. Sheep and goats bleated, their bells ringing as they moved and the youngsters tasted dust and sand in their mouths.

"I'm scared," Fatima whimpered again, holding tightly to Sienna. "What's happening? Where's the cemetery?"

She looked up fearfully at the huge creatures next to them. Abruptly, as if released from a catapult, Luca shot from the door stumbling into them and falling to his knees.

"I was trying to hide inside the tomb when some sort of force pushed me against the door and I couldn't move," he stuttered. "I was paralysed." Sweat dripped down his face.

"But was does it mean?" Sienna asked. "Is this real or are we dreaming?"

Two sets of topaz eyes as bright as the sun regarded them, making the youngsters avert their faces and shade them with a hand. Seeing the beasts open their huge mouths, the children shrank together, putting up their other hand to protect themselves, squealing their fear.

"We are the guardians of the dead. We protect them and their passage into the next world." The sphinxes' voices were as soft as velvet but steely, like a kid glove in a gauntlet.

"Anyone trying to break the seal into the tomb is transported here and given a riddle. If it isn't solved by sundown, they stay as sacrifices for the Gods."

Fatima began to tremble. She didn't want to be sacrificed! She was no good at riddles and it wasn't her who'd tried to break into a tomb. "It's your fault Luca," she cried, tears spilling down her face, "trying to scare us and now look! We're going to be eaten or killed!"

Luca was almost crying too. "I'm sorry," he mumbled. "It was just a bit of fun."

The sphinxes watched, impassive.

"But why?" Sienna demanded, putting her arms around Fatima. "Why are people transported?"

"To teach them not to meddle," came the reply. This made Fatima cry even more. "I wasn't meddling," Luca began to say but Sienna cut him off.

"None of us want to sacrificed!" she declared. "So it's no use crying or blaming each other! That won't get us out of here!"

Looking up, she stared through her fingers into the topaz eyes that blazed with anticipation of an easy prey.

"So, what's the riddle?" Sienna demanded.

"What has one voice, yet becomes four-footed, two footed then three-footed?"

"Eh?" Luca exclaimed.

"We're never going to get it." Fatima started to sniffle again.

"It doesn't make sense!" Luca complained. Sienna tried to calm both of them, suggesting that they get their thinking caps on.

The sphinxes said nothing more, turning their heads to stare at the distant horizon.

III

The heat had made them all sticky and fractious.

"We have to come up with ideas!" Sienna ordered.

"I'm getting a headache," Fatima complained. "I need a drink. I can't think straight." Opening her bottle, she sobbed, "Maybe it'll be my last drink."

"Don't be daft, Fatima. We'll be out of this in no time," Sienna encouraged. "And you're good at coming up with ideas."

They stood, rattling their brains, trying not to think about what would happen if they didn't solve the riddle.

"Everything has one voice, doesn't it?" Fatima said, snuffling quietly.

"No," Luca replied. "A tree doesn't, a building doesn't." He began fiddling in his school rucksack.

"True. So let's think of animals and people then," Sienna said. "But then not all animals have four feet, or two or three." Seeing Luca messing with something in his hand, she said to him. "Are you going to help or just muck about?"

"I was trying my phone," he waved it in front of her, "to see if I could get a signal -,"

"What for?" Fatima exploded. "A take-away? We're in the middle of a nightmare *you* started -"

"To see if I could get on the internet," Luca shouted, "to see if we could find the answer to the riddle! It's bound to be there somewhere."

"Did you get one?" When Luca shook his head, she laughed, "Ha! Thought so." Sienna wanted to knock their heads together. This wasn't helping.

"Luca we need to be practical. I reckon we've got about an hour or so left," she pointed between the sphinxes at the sun, which was now lying low in the sky. "Time seems to be different here, it'll be dusk soon. So *concentrate*, both of you!"

IV

They went through all the four, three and two-footed animals they could think of.

"A four-footed animal could become three-footed if it broke a leg," Luca suggested.

"Yeh, but it wouldn't be able to walk if it broke two legs, would it?" Fatima answered.

"Well, gorillas walk on two legs," Luca argued, "and they also crawl on their arms. So that's two parts of the riddle solved."

"That's good, but we still don't have the three-legged bit sorted." Sienna was frustrated. Somewhere in her head was the answer. She was sure she'd heard the riddle before.

As they debated, the heat that had made their clothes cling to them began to cool; the sounds of camels and sheep quietened and instead of spice smells, there was now the aroma of cooking and fires.

Shadows began to lengthen and darken the entrance

where they stood. Fatima began to cry again.

"We're going to be sacrificed," she wailed. "I'm never going to see mum or dad again! They'll be so upset, never being able to find me." She began sobbing.

"Don't be such a baby!" Luca hotly responded. "We'll never get out if - ,"

"That's it!" Sienna cried triumphantly.

"That's what?" her friends chorused.

"Baby! Four-footed, becomes two-footed! Of course!" Sienna began to dance around. Luca and Fatima looked at each other, afraid that the stress had sent Sienna mad.

"You're not making sense," Fatima said, putting her hands on Sienna's arms to stop her dancing. "What do you mean?"

The sphinxes heads turned toward them again.

"You have sixty seconds to give an answer before the sun sets." The velvety voices purred, topaz eyes sent out blazing sparks, tails swished and claws flexed in anticipation of more sacrifices to their Gods.

"Join hands," Sienna ordered. "Quickly!"

Fatima trembled. Luca tensed. Sienna took a deep breath and looked up.

"A man has one voice. He's four-legged when he crawls

as a baby, two-legged as an adult and three-legged when an old man with a walking stick!"

Everyone held their breaths. A hiss escaped from the sphinxes, their gaze grew in intensity, making the children so hot, they feared they would burst into flames. Then a whoosh of cold air and a dark shadow passed over them.

V

Quivering, squeezing each other's hands, they stood immobile, expecting a mouth or a claw to attack them. When nothing happened, they squinted through half-open eyelids. Above them was a full moon, shining directly into their eyes. It lit up the tomb where they were like a spotlight on a stage.

Wonderingly, they looked around. The sphinxes were once more grey statues and behind them the tomb had returned to its usual size and colour. They breathed out, sobbing with relief, hugging each other.

"Did we just dream that?" Luca asked. "Did we or didn't we just visit Egypt or somewhere?"

"I don't know," Sienna answered. "Maybe we did. I don't want to do it again though."

"Me neither," Fatima said, still trembling. "We were lucky you got the answer. How did you know?"

"Greek myths!" Sienna laughed shakily. "I knew I'd heard it before."

"Do you think these are all time-portals?" Luca pointed to the other tombs around the cemetery. The girls shrugged, not caring, just glad to be back in a place they knew.

"I know I'm never going to try to get in one again," Luca continued. "*And* I'm only going to walk through here in daylight."

Fatima got out her phone to look at the time "It's only five o'clock," she said to the others. "But weren't we away for a day? And how can there be a full moon?"

"Don't know," Sienna replied. "But we'll have to wriggle though the locked gates now!" Grabbing her bag, she linked arms with both friends.

"What'll we say about getting back late?" Fatima asked.

"You can tell them," Sienna said, "That we were working on our creative writing piece for school but time swallowed us up!" Laughing together, they setting off down the path, lit by the full moon.

The sphinxes gazed after them, their topaz eyes glowing.

Turn the page for the start of

A Mixenden Mystery

featuring in

Strange Tales in Calderdale

Book 3 in the Strange Tales series

Available 2016

A Mixenden Mystery

I

"Mary lass, we're off now. Don't forget to baste the meat and collect the fat for later."

"No missus, ah won't." Mary bobbed her knees in a curtsey as the Master and Mistress of Mixenden Old Hall donned their outdoor clothing for the early trek to the church at Halifax.

Watching as the pair set off on the cart, Mary smiled to herself. It was a good eight miles there and back, and with a Sunday sermon lasting at least a couple of hours, it meant she had the house all to herself until at least three o'clock.

She could take her time doing the household chores and fixing the dinner.

Looking out of the small-paned leaded windows at the fields and woods as she washed the breakfast platters, Mary thought about how lucky she was to be working in such a lovely house, nestling as it was in the valley.

A sturdy place with panelled rooms, flagged floors and large inglenook fireplaces, the building had seen its ups and downs. Mary knew about the visitations of the priest hunters. She never ventured into the hole where the priests had been hidden, fearful of what ghosts might be lurking there, having heard of the tortures some of them underwent.

But she put that from her mind, enjoying her role and glad that it was only an hour's walk from her family. She pictured them working away on their looms and was grateful again that at fourteen she'd got a job as a maid at the Hall. True, they were long days but as not as long or hard as working in spinning and weaving like her family did.

Humming as she swept with the besom, dusting, chopping vegetables, putting the beef onto roast in front of the blazing kitchen fire – not forgetting the fat pan beneath – Mary dawdled, enjoying the freedom of the house, imagining she was the mistress. In such a way, hours passed and a watery sunshine lit the dim interiors as she moved around the bedrooms.

Mary was smoothing down bedsheets when she heard a loud rapping on the door. This was very unusual on a Sunday when families were all at church, so she clattered down the staircase thinking it might be an emergency. Unlocking the big wooden door, Mary opened it cautiously as she'd been taught, for you could never be too careful.

II

On the threshold was a man of about twenty with damp hair clinging to his face, dishevelled clothing, muddy boots and a very tired look about him.

"Ey lass," he said, "I'm reet sorry t'disturb ye on t'Sabbath, but I've traipsed ower yon moors from near Bolton Abbey and I'm weary an' footsore. Ah were wonderin' if tha could spare a poor traveller a bit o'snap afore ah go on?"

He looked so forlorn that Mary couldn't help but take pity on him. It was no wonder he looked muddy and messy if he'd come all that way in a morning, it was a tidy step across those lonely tracks. With his brown hair and green eyes, he reminded her of her late older brother who she missed all the time, so she decided that she'd offer the traveller some shelter.

Ushering him in, Mary said, "You do look nithered. Come t'fire an' warm thissen. I'm sure I can find you a bite t'eat an' a sup o'summat." She led him to the rocking chair at the side of the fire, where the meat was roasting on a spit.

"Ah'd be mighty grateful," he said as he lowered himself into the chair. "Ah declare ahm so famished ah could eat a cow!" He smiled and his eyes crinkled, reminding Mary even more of her dead brother.

She smiled back, thinking what a nice man he seemed. Bustling around, Mary cut some bread, found a piece of cheese and poured out a small beer which she brought to him on a board. Turning the spit whilst he ate, she saw how he savoured every morsel.

"Tha dunt mind if ah tek me ease for a short while an' have forty winks, does tha? So's ah can dry out a bit?"

"Nay sir," Mary responded. "I can clean an' get on wi' me chores whilst thee has a kip."

She left him by the fireside and continued getting the dinner ready for the Master and Mistress's return. Glancing at the man from time to time, she saw him slowly slide down in the chair, his legs stretched to the hearth for warmth.

As usual, Mary fell to dreaming, wondering why the man had been at the Abbey, whether he was an itinerant pedlar - though he didn't have any bag or box with him - or even if he was travelling to meet a sweetheart at a secret tryst.

A noise behind her brought her from her reverie. Looking round, she saw the man slumped in the rocking chair, his mouth slack as he snored loudly. 'Poor dear,' she thought, 'he must be exhausted.' As she gazed at him, the man shifted and so did the girl's stomach. His cloak had opened revealing a pistol in his belt!

III

Staring in horror, Mary's heart beat uncomfortably, her mind racing. What did she know of him? How foolish had she been letting him in just because he reminded her of her brother. Where had he really come from? What if he was a thief come to rob the house of its treasures? There were armed gangs around who thought nothing of attacking and killing someone who got in their way.

Mary could feel bile rising in her throat. She was frantic. What should she do? She was only fourteen and small for her age, not strong enough to fight off a man intent on murder.

Scanning the kitchen, searching for an implement she could use to defend herself, her eyes lighted on the pan under the roasting meat. It was half-full of hot sizzling fat. Flicking her eyes between the pan and the man, from whose open mouth snoring continued, Mary made a decision. Grabbing a cloth, she tiptoed to the fat pan and lifted it as quietly as she could.

Moving slowly and stealthily to the sleeping figure, she halted before him. Holding her breath, she positioned the pan above the man's gaping mouth and tipped the red hot contents down his throat.

Immediately, with a strangled bubbling scream, the man leapt into the air clutching his throat, the smell of burning flesh filling the air.

Strange Tales in Calderdale *available 2016*

FUN ACTIVITIES

Protect yourself against a Boggart

Have iron objects, like scissors and fire pokers in the house or nails in a pocket. These can protect against a boggart settling in or following.

Farmers should put yellow flowers and rowan berries in front of the door and inside a barn or byre.

Rowan crosses on Mayday Eve and Midsummer Eve are a good way of stopping boggarts, hobs, faeries and sprites doing mischief as they're more active on those days.

Salt, yellow flowers and twigs from the rowan tree (or mountain ash) are also very powerful charms.

Draw a picture of a Stone Head and a Phantom Carriage and Driver

Wordsearch

L	N	N	K	A	O	S	R	M	C
L	A	N	A	C	I	L	O	E	U
E	L	D	E	R	E	T	L	T	N
W	L	N	O	P	N	T	W	B	N
K	U	A	C	A	I	F	E	S	I
N	K	R	H	C	U	L	M	D	N
I	S	P	H	I	N	X	A	E	W
P	C	E	M	E	T	E	R	Y	O
S	A	D	G	K	E	R	A	N	M
D	W	R	H	U	C	W	O	U	A
T	H	E	A	T	R	E	B	A	N
G	T	R	A	G	G	O	B	H	D

Words can go forwards, backwards and diagonally.

Boar	Celtic Head	Phantom
Boggart	Elder	Spinkwell
Cemetery	Oak	Sphinx
Cunning Woman	Olicana	Theatre

There are two other words. Can you find them?

111

Did you know?

- Some freshly-picked rosemary simmered in a pint of water for 15 minutes, then cooled, makes a fantastic rinse for dark hair. If you have fair hair, use chamomile instead.

- In the Domesday Book (1086), Bradford is a village with outlying hamlets and manors. Gamel, a man of Norse descent, was the biggest landowner

- 'To be on tenterhooks' comes from hanging cloth to dry on a wooden frame called a 'tenter'. These had hooks of bent nails from which the cloth was hung to make sure it didn't shrink as it dried. Today, being on 'tenterhooks' means not knowing what's going to happen, waiting for an answer.

- Normans came from the North as in 'Northman' or Norseman. Norman is an anagram of Roman.

- Bram Stoker, the author of Dracula was the manager of the great Victorian actor Henry Irving, who died at the Midland Hotel in Bradford in 1905. Irving's ghost is said to haunt the hotel.

- 'Put t'wood in t'oil' means 'Close the door!

Story inspiration

1. The Boar's Severed Head

There are several versions of the legend of how the last wild boar of Bradford was killed, spanning the 10th to the 14th century. It's why there's a boar's head on the Bradford Coat of Arms. But no one knows if any of them are really true, so Ranulf, Aleycia and Agnes the cunning woman could have been responsible!

If you look closely when walking around the city centre, you'll spot lots of boars' heads on buildings, bollards and signposts. You can visit what is reputed to be the Boar's Well along a green-way that may be part of the old Cliff Wood. It takes you past the Spinkwell, which people visited in Victorian times to 'take the water'. You can also see a boar's head at Bolling Hall, named after the Lord of the Manor featured in the story, which is a very spooky place, well worth a visit.

http://www.bees-ymca.org.uk/places_boarswell

http://www.bradfordmuseums.org/venues/bolling-hall

2. A Boggart in the Beck

Bradford Beck runs through Bradford city centre, down to Shipley where it joins the River Aire. There are many other becks that flow down the hills, which is one reason the area was known as Bradford Dale. It's said that shepherds discovered that the soft water was good for washing fleeces and wool and settled here.

Over time, mills developed along these waterways especially during the Industrial Revolution.

But myth tells us that brownies and boggarts have lived here for a long, long time, possibly brought by ancient tribes. There are many Yorkshire tales of boggarts plaguing houses, farms and mills which have been handed down. This one's inspired by a couple of stories: one that's been retold for years and another related to me by an elderly mill worker.

3. A Ride to the Death

I walked past old mounting blocks several times a week as a child and was fascinated by them, wondering about the old carriages that would have stopped to pick up passengers when Bradford was still a mainly rural place and the turnpike roads were being made. I lived near an ancient wood with a track-way that linked towns and villages, which carriages used almost two hundred years ago. I played in the wood and it could be very spooky. This story links those childhood fancies. The wood and the blocks are still there.

4. Playing in the Park

Bradford Town (now City) Hall's design was based on a building in Florence, Italy and was finished in 1873. It has statues from William the Conqueror to Queen Victoria made by the firm Farmer and Brindley. It's always amazed me how so few people notice them; they hurry past, rarely looking up at the wonderful work. These Kings and Queens had an impact on our national and local history, especially in the civil war. Each statue is draped in costume of the time and they have great expressions. They overlook the location of Bradford Beck (now covered) the waterway responsible for Broad Ford's development. And now with the mirror pool, water is again a feature in the centre. As I write, there are plaques being carved that will be placed on city centre pavements to show where Bradford Beck flows. www.bradford-beck.org

5. Heads It Is

During the 1970s, many carved stone heads were found around Yorkshire, several in the Bradford area. Some looked very old and it was thought they were from Celtic times. Director of Bradford Museums' Service, Sidney Jackson documented over 600 and had an exhibition of them. But further research showed that many of the 'heads' were 17th century and later in origin, and were used to ward of evil spirits (see John Billingsley's 'The Stony Gaze'). Historians still argue about whether the Celts 'cult of the head' really existed or if heads were simply for decoration. Whatever the answer, there are many heads that can be seen on churches, in wells, on houses, inns, barns and walls, as well as rock at the sides of rivers.

6. Theatrical Spirits

As an actor, I've 'trod the boards' at many theatres and they always have a ghost story or two. The Bradford Playhouse is no exception. The area its in has changed many times through the centuries from landscaped grounds of a big house to a centre for merchants involved in the wool trade (Little Germany). There was once a Quaker graveyard from which bodies were moved during building work. This story is based on tales from fellow actors and the theatre's archive, as well as personal experiences.

7. Secret of the Sphinxes

Undercliffe Cemetery was next to my middle school and I'd spend hours wandering around, reading names on gravestones and making up stories about them. A fascinating place (which you may have seen in films and TV programmes) with lots of tombs, tall monuments and some gravestones that have no names. It's the resting place of many of the people who made Bradford into the wealthy place it was in the 19th and early 20th century. I was always interested with the sphinxes outside one of the tombs, which are one of the inspirations for the story. This year I made a short video about the cemetery:

https://m.youtube.com/watch?v=kJqG3a5pDbk

http://undercliffecemetery.co.uk/

Glossary

Amphora A type of container with a distinctive shape and size, made as early as Neolithic times

Boggart A hob, goblin, evil or malicious. Found mostly in Northern England and Scotland

Bollywood Name of popular Indian film industry. Many films have spectacular song and dance routines

Brigantes Name given to the Celtic tribes in pre-Roman times who controlled what became Northern England

Brownie A small good-natured brown elf or imp who secretly helps at with household chores

Cans Headphones used to communicate between the backstage crew with technical team in a theatre

Celtic Head Many carved stone heads have been found in Yorkshire, some in Bradford. It's thought that they were part of the religion of the Iron Age and earlier. Placing them so water could flow over them may be part of a ritual for people to talk with water Gods

Circle Upper tier of seats in a theatre

Circlet	A circle or ring worn on the head as an ornament or crown
Coif	A close-fitting cap that covers the top, back, and sides of the head. Worn by men and women; still worn by nuns under veils
Cottar	A peasant farmer or a tenant renting land from a farmer or landlord
Cunning Woman	Cunning also means knowledgeable or wise and comes from an Old English word 'ken', which means 'to know'. A person who, healed, created herbal remedies, provided charms, anti-witch measures, spells, and fortune telling services
Eboracum	Roman name for York
Desk	A piece of equipment in a theatre or venue from which lights, sounds and movement can be controlled
Dryad	A tree nymph, or tree spirit
Flytower	This is a place in a theatre where there is a system of ropes, pulleys and counterweights which mean a stage crew can quickly, quietly and safely fly curtains, lights, scenery, stage effects and even people in and out of view of the audience
Fuller	A person who washes or scours woollen cloth

Fuller's Earth	A clay like substance (aluminium silicate) used for centuries to remove dirt and oil before woollen cloth was completed
Galliard	A form of dance popular in the 16th century. Elizabeth 1st is said to have danced galliards as her morning exercise
Green Man	An ancient God or natural spirit who protects the forests and plants
Green Room	Another name for a waiting room and for performers before and after after a show
Mardy	A Yorkshire word for being 'moody'.
Mic	Microphone
Neolithic	Late Stone Age period
Olicana	Roman name for Ilkley
Piecer	Someone in a mill who pieces broken threads together
Posset	A hot drink of milk curdled with wine or ale, often flavoured with spices
Quiver	A case for arrows, carried over the shoulder
Scavenge	To clean under looms, spinning and weaving machines. A 'scavenger', was usually a small child
Salve	An ointment used to help the skin to heal
Scour	To wash wool to take out dirt, grease especially using fast flowing water

Shape-shifter	Something or someone who can change what/who they are, eg from a brownie to a boggart
Shire	A county in Great Britain
Soapwort	A plant that can be used to make a lather. Latin name, Saponaria but has lots of different names across the country
Sphinx	A figure of an imaginary creature having the head of a man, woman or animal and the body of a lion. In both Egyptian and Greek mythology. The Sphinx of Thebes posed the riddle of the three ages of man to Oedipus. When he solved it, the sphinx killed itself
Stalls	The lower seats in a theatre
Technician	Someone who makes the lights, sound and scenery work in a theatre, music event, etc
Tenterfield	A place where woollen cloth was stretched with hooks to dry after fulling
Torque	The bronze, gilded or gold neck ring worn by Celtic men (also torq, torc)
Wapentake	Parts of Yorkshire were divided into these for governing, a bit like councils today

ACTIVITIES - ANSWERS

Wordsearch

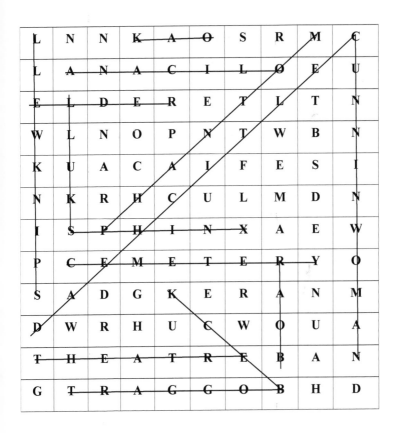

L	N	N	K	A	O	S	R	M	C
L	A	N	A	C	I	L	O	E	U
E	L	D	E	R	E	T	L	T	N
W	L	N	O	P	N	T	W	B	N
K	U	A	C	A	I	F	E	S	I
N	K	R	H	C	U	L	M	D	N
I	S	P	H	I	N	X	A	E	W
P	C	E	M	E	T	E	R	Y	O
S	A	D	G	K	E	R	A	N	M
D	W	R	H	U	C	W	O	U	A
T	H	E	A	T	R	E	B	A	N
G	T	R	A	G	G	O	B	H	D

Missing Words: Beck, Skull

About the Illustrator: Clare Lindley

This is Clare's second book cover design. She specialized in illustration doing graphic design at Bradford College but papercutting wasn't one of the subjects; she 'fell into by accident' and loved it. Her beautiful pieces are inspired by the Yorkshire landscape; its four legged and winged inhabitants fuel Clare's imagination, reflected in the intricate designs and bold images in her work, like the cover. Work is hand- produced using a scalpel and black paper: when a piece is finished, if she decides that colour would improve it, further layers of coloured paper are added; no painting is involved. Recently she began doing small designs for jewellery, notebooks and hanging ornaments.

Clare's exhibited widely in the UK and internationally, especially in Canada and the US. She's a member of the Guild of American Papercutters (a piece of hers is in their museum collection), and she also co-runs an online gallery, Arts Tarts.

Clare's available for commissions if it fits with her style and way of working.

www.papercuttergirl.co.uk
www.**arttarts**.co.uk

Acknowledgements

Being a Bradford lass, I've known many of the legends from being a child thanks to my primary school teachers, the local studies library and visits to museums. When I was involved with Bradford Playhouse, many people related tales of their 'spooky' experiences and I had some of my own too. Thanks also go to Friends of Bradford's Becks who suggested places along the becks where boggarts might be found; to Bradford Industrial Museum and their learning team; to my Gran, who worked in mills all her life; to Steve Bottoms and Ros Garside and Bradford Libraries who provided an opportunity to test the tales. Big thanks to the children and families who listened, participated and commented at Bradford and Saltaire Festivals, which has helped to shape the stories.

And of course thanks to Clare Lindley for her fabulous papercut illustrations which never fail to amaze me.

Last but not least, very big thanks go to Tony for his patience, support, suggestions, comments, photography and for listening to each stage of the development of the stories.

www.word-sauce.com

Ordering

Books are available in selected bookshops (see website), can be ordered direct from Gizmo Publications:

irene.lofthouse@btinternet.com
irene.lofthouse@gmail.com

Details of postage and packing for orders, multiple orders and overseas orders are on the site.

102 Harrogate Street, Bradford, BD3 0LE

Also available on Amazon